LKNER'S

STORIES

NOTES

including
- *Life and Background of the Author*
- *An Introduction to Yoknapatawpha County*
- *Critical Commentaries*
    "A Rose for Emily"
    "That Evening Sun"
    "Barn Burning"
    "Dry September"
    "Spotted Horses"
- *Critical Essay*
    Faulkner's Style
- *Review Questions and Essay Topics*
- *Faulkner's Published Works*
- *Selected Bibliography*

by
James L. Roberts, Ph.D.
University of Nebraska–Lincoln

INCORPORATED
LINCOLN, NEBRASKA 68501

Editor	Consulting Editor
Gary Carey, M.A. *University of Colorado*	*James L. Roberts, Ph.D.* *Department of English* *University of Nebraska*

CONTENTS

CONTENTS

FAULKNER'S SHORT STORIES

Notes

LIFE AND BACKGROUND OF THE AUTHOR

Reading William Faulkner's short stories is an excellent way to approach his major works. Although his novels are better known and more widely read, many of the same characters and ideas found in them are introduced in his stories.

Faulkner was born in New Albany, Mississippi, on September 25, 1897, but soon thereafter his family moved to Oxford, Mississippi, a site he would rename Jefferson in his fiction and would use as the setting for almost all of his novels and short stories.

Faulkner came from an old, proud, and distinguished Mississippi family, which included a governor, a colonel in the Confederate Army, and notable business pioneers. His great-grandfather, Colonel William Clark Falkner (the "u" was added to Faulkner's name by mistake when his first novel was published, and he retained the misspelling), emigrated from Tennessee to Mississippi during the first part of the nineteenth century. Colonel Falkner, who appears as Colonel John Sartoris in Faulkner's fiction, had a distinguished career as a soldier, both in the Mexican War and the American Civil War. During the Civil War, his fiery temper caused him to be demoted from colonel to lieutenant colonel.

Falkner was heavily involved in events taking place during Reconstruction, the twelve years following the end of the Civil War in 1865, when the Union governed the secessional Confederate states before readmitting them. He killed several men during this time and became a rather notorious figure. With a partner, he oversaw the financing and construction of the first post-Civil War railroad in the South; then, after quarreling with his partner, the relationship dissolved. When this former business associate ran for the state legislature, Falkner ran against him and soundly defeated him.

Once asked how much he based his characterization of the genteel Colonel Sartoris on his great-grandfather, Faulkner responded:

> That's difficult to say. That comes back to what we spoke of—the three sources the writer draws from—and I myself would have to stop and go page by page to see just how much I drew from family annals that I had listened to from these old undefeated spinster aunts that children of my time grew up with. Probably, well, the similarity of raising of that infantry regiment, that was the same, the—his death was about—was pretty close, pretty close parallel, but the rest of it I would have to go through to—page by page and remember, did I hear this or did I imagine this?

What does not appear in Faulkner's fiction is that during all of his great-grandfather's projects and designs, the colonel took time to write one of the nation's bestsellers, *The White Rose of Memphis*, which was published in book form in 1881. He also wrote two other novels, but only *The White Rose of Memphis* was successful.

Falkner was finally killed by one of his rivals, and his death was never avenged. Today, a statue of him stands in the Oxford, Mississippi, cemetery. Dressed in a Confederate uniform, he looks out over the region for which he fought so desperately and so valiantly. Only William Faulkner, of all the Falkner clan, is as distinguished— and, ultimately, became more distinguished—than his great-grandfather.

Faulkner's personal life fits seemingly into the romantic cliché of what a writer's life is like, and he often contributed deliberately to the various stories circulating about him. For example, in 1919, during the final months of World War I, he was rejected for service in the U.S. Armed Forces because he was too short. Not easily deterred, he went to Canada and was accepted into the Royal Canadian Air Force, but World War I ended before he finished his training. Returning to Oxford, he adopted an English accent and walked around his hometown in a Royal Canadian Air Force uniform, which he had purchased, along with some medals to adorn the uniform.

To write about Faulkner's personal life is to put oneself at risk of not being able to separate the facts from the imaginary life he conceived for himself. Critics generally agree that he did not graduate from high school, and that he dropped out of the University of Mississippi after a couple of years. He moved to New York City's Greenwich Village at the invitation of an established Mississippi writer, Stark Young, who used his influence to get Faulkner a position as a bookstore clerk, but he returned to Oxford after a few months. He then traveled to New Orleans, where he got a job running a boat that carried bootleg liquor. There, he met the established American writer Sherwood Anderson, author of *Winesburg, Ohio*. Observing the leisurely life Anderson led, Faulkner decided that he wanted to become a writer, and Anderson helped get his first novel, *Soldiers' Pay* (1926), published—with the promise that he would never have to read it.

Because *Soldiers' Pay* was not successful commercially, Faulkner again was forced to find employment. This time, however, he found an ideal job: He shipped out as a deck hand on a freighter bound for Europe, where he spent many weeks loafing about the Mediterranean, especially in France and in Italy. His own imaginative reports of his life abroad have never been corroborated.

In 1929, Faulkner married Estelle Oldham Franklin, a high-school sweetheart who had been married previously, and he began a period of serious writing. Over the next few years, three of his greatest novels—*The Sound and the Fury* (1929), *As I Lay Dying* (1930), and *Light in August* (1932)—were published. Despite his numerous publications, however, he still did not earn enough money to support his and Estelle's lifestyle. In 1933, a daughter, Jill, was born, and by the mid-1930s, Faulkner was deeply troubled with debt: In addition to his own family and servants, he supported his brother Dean's children after Dean died in a plane crash, in a plane Faulkner had bought for him.

Mounting financial problems forced Faulkner to publish short stories as quickly as he could, and he finally capitulated to the monetary rewards of working as a screenwriter in Hollywood for a thousand dollars a week. He hated the work, but he returned to it off and on during the 1930s, working long enough to pay off his significant debts, and then returning to Oxford, where he wrote at least three novels—*Absalom, Absalom!* (1936), *The Wild Palms* (1939), and *The Hamlet* (1940), in addition to several short stories.

Despite Faulkner's having produced some of the finest twentieth-century novels, his early works were never commercial successes; the exception is *Sanctuary* (1931), at first thought to be a sensational potboiler but later viewed otherwise. He struggled financially until the 1948 publication of *Intruder in the Dust*. The novel was made into a movie, filmed in Oxford, and Faulkner found himself an important figure in and around the town, the same town that earlier had spurned him, calling him such names as "Count No 'Count."

When Faulkner won the Nobel Prize for literature in 1949, only one of his novels was in print. Almost overnight, he was acclaimed by critics, writers, teachers, and reporters. From being an obscure, backwoods country writer, he was catapulted suddenly to the highest echelons of literary achievement. He took advantage of this newfound acclaim by encouraging young writers not to quit their craft. In his Nobel Prize acceptance speech, he seized the spotlight of worldwide attention "as a pinnacle from which I might be listened to by the young men and women already dedicated to the same anguish and travail, among whom is already that one who will some day stand here where I am standing."

In 1957, Faulkner accepted a position as writer-in-residence at the University of Virginia. There, in informal class settings, he answered many questions about his novels and his artistic vision. Although he sometimes confused aspects of one novel with another, his answers attest to his characters' vibrant personalities and expand on his panoramic vision for the Yoknapatawpha saga.

In June 1962, Faulkner was thrown from his horse and injured his back. He suffered intense pain and was admitted to Wright's Sanitarium, in Byhalia, Mississippi, on July 5. The next day—ironically the date of the old Colonel's birthday—he died, leaving behind him a body of work unsurpassed in twentieth-century literature.

Faulkner uses new techniques to express man's position in the modern world. The complexity of his narrative structures mirrors the complex lives we lead. Most of his novels and short stories probe into the mores and morals of the South, which he was not hesitant to criticize. In his early fiction, Faulkner views despairingly man's position in the universe. He briefly voices this same sense of futility and defeat in his Nobel Prize acceptance speech: "Our tragedy today is a general and universal physical fear so long sustained by now that we can even bear it. There are no longer problems of the spirit.

There is only the question: When will I be blown up?" Man is a weak creature incapable of rising above his selfish needs.

In his latter works, however, Faulkner's tone changes, and he emphasizes humankind's survival. He believes human beings to be potentially great, affirming that "man shall not only endure: he will prevail. He is immortal, not because he alone among creatures has an inexhaustible voice, but because he has a soul, a spirit capable of compassion and sacrifice and endurance." Penetrating deeply the psychological motivations for human beings' actions, Faulkner concludes that hope remains for our salvation from despair.

AN INTRODUCTION TO YOKNAPATAWPHA COUNTY

In his third novel, *Flags in the Dust*, Faulkner created a mythological Mississippi county and named it Yoknapatawpha (**Yawk**-naw-puh-**toff**-uh), with its county seat in Jefferson. This particular novel, however, was not published during Faulkner's lifetime; it appeared posthumously in 1973. What did appear in 1929 was a heavily edited and much shorter version of *Flags in the Dust*, renamed *Sartoris* to emphasize the importance of one of the county's major families, the Sartorises.

The county of Yoknapatawpha and its county seat of Jefferson are based on the real county of Jefferson, Mississippi, and its county seat of Oxford. The name "Yoknapatawpha" is derived from authentic Native American names found on old maps of Jefferson County. In 1936, Faulkner drew a map of his fictional county, showing where various scenes from his novels and short stories take place, and he first included the map in *Absalom, Absalom!*, published that same year. The creation of this mythological county is one of modern literature's greatest feats.

Many of Faulkner's same characters are found in his various novels; a character who appears in a minor role in one novel might reappear as a significant character in another. For example, a Snopes appears briefly in the first novel of the Yoknapatawpha series, and Faulkner comments that this Snopes is one of an inexhaustible number of Snopeses who have invaded the county. Later in his career, the Snopes family becomes the subject of three different novels and many short stories. His other characters appear and reappear in varying roles, and, therefore, in reading more than one of his novels or short stories, we come to know a great deal about the diverse people who inhabit Yoknapatawpha County.

The Southern Aristocracy. The aristocracy of Yoknapatawpha County is represented by Colonel John Sartoris and his family, the General Jason Compson family, Major de Spain, and the Griersons. Because members of the Sartoris family appear more frequently than do the other members of the aristocracy, Colonel Sartoris best represents this class.

Sartoris appears as a major or minor character in many Faulkner short stories, including "A Rose for Emily," in which he tells Miss Emily that she does not have to pay the taxes on her property; in "Barn Burning," Colonel Sartoris ("Sarty") Snopes, named for the genteel colonel, is the only ethical Snopes in the entire county. Because Colonel John Sartoris epitomizes Southern values—gallantry, generosity, hospitality, valor, pride, honor, and a dedication to the protection of the region's ideals—in "Barn Burning," when young Sarty Snopes is called to testify before the Justice of the Peace and gives his name as "Colonel Sartoris Snopes," the Justice says, "I reckon anybody named for Colonel Sartoris in this country can't help but tell the truth, can they?"

Although the colonel is the most admired man in Yoknapatawpha County and best represents the values associated with the Old South, he is also one of the most difficult people to get along with. At the beginning of the Civil War, he is the first man to raise a regiment to fight the Yankees. But within a year, he is voted out of his command because of his arrogance and intolerance. He returns to Yoknapatawpha County and organizes his own troop of "irregulars." As the leader of this troop, he becomes somewhat of an instant legend; he seems to be always in the local vicinity or in the neighboring land, protecting the women and children left defenseless while their menfolk are off fighting.

Colonel Sartoris is also admired for his cleverness and ambition. Once, with only a few men, he unexpectedly rides upon an encampment of about sixty Yankees, but his innovative reaction is superb: Pretending to have a large number of troops surrounding the Yankees, he yells commands to make-believe lieutenants, demanding that the Yankees surrender. Afterward, he takes their food and their rifles, and he makes them strip down to their underwear. He then pretends to relax his guard, allowing the prisoners to escape in small groups. This way, they think that they have outwitted him and his regiment, never realizing that the colonel has only a few men with him.

Supremely self-assured and exuding confidence in everything he does, the absolute and undeviating loyalty that Sartoris inspires among the men in his regiment attests to his ability to lead with authority and respect. The fact that his arrogance causes his demotion in his official capacity does not detract from the fact that, as the commander of his own troop, he receives extraordinary loyalty and devotion from his fellow rebels.

The colonel also inspires men's confidences in matters other than wartime tactics. At the end of the war, he is broke and destitute, but he dreams of building a railroad. He is able to communicate that dream to others and convince enough of them to finance the project—not just once, but again and again—so that the railroad, and even the first engine, are built with capital from others. Although Colonel Sartoris himself has no money, he has a vision and a dream. Most important, he is a determined man who refuses to be vanquished—by anything or anyone.

The Snopeses.   During his writing career, Faulkner wrote numerous short stories featuring members of the Snopes family. He also wrote a trilogy of three novels—*The Hamlet*, *The Town*, and *The Mansion*—that has the Snopes family as the central concern. Throughout the trilogy, he often revised his short stories about the Snopeses and included them in the novels.

As a class of people, the Snopeses are the antithesis of the highbrow society represented by Colonel Sartoris. Whereas Sartoris is refined and carries about himself an Old World gentility, the Snopeses are crass, poor, and ill-mannered. V. K. Ratliff, the narrator of "Spotted Horses," sums up the Snopeses' shady character with the deceptively simple saying, "Them Snopes," an expression that underscores the astonishment and exasperation of Yoknapatawpha County's citizens viewing the Snopeses' behavior.

The Snopeses are best represented by Flem, who in "Spotted Horses" symbolizes the rise of an amoral materialism that will eventually overpower all other moral values. He is the elemental and destructive force of invincible greed opposed to all other forces in Faulkner's fiction, and he accomplishes his ends with a perverse and distorted vitality. The Snopeses' ubiquitous inhumanity infiltrates every aspect of the community life, and their calculating and dehumanizing exploits leave their victims stupefied and in abject rage.

Singularly, the descendants of Abner Snopes, who in "Barn Burning" epitomizes the single-mindedness of his family, are inveterate liars, thieves, murderers, blackmailers, and the personification of every type of treachery. As a clan, they present an insurmountable and insidious example of the horrors of materialistic aggrandizement, and they accomplish their aims with complete, unshakable calm. They are so impersonal that their gruesome inhumanity must be viewed in a comic manner. When we cease to view the Snopeses with ironic and humorous detachment, we lose all perspective. In "Spotted Horses," it is almost impossible to define our reaction to Flem Snopes' audacious gift—"A little sweetening for the chaps"—to Mrs. Armstid, except to agree with Ratliff that if he himself were to do what Flem does, he would be lynched.

Flem and his spotted horses represent the infiltration of unorthodox behavior into a heretofore serene community life. The disorder that he causes forms the basic pattern of his strategy. He does not pit himself against the community in personal combat; rather, he incites diverse elements within the community to battle each other. His last name symbolizes everything unprincipled and amoral in society.

CRITICAL COMMENTARIES

"A ROSE FOR EMILY"

Faulkner's most famous, most popular, and most anthologized short story, "A Rose for Emily" evokes the terms Southern gothic and grotesque, two types of literature in which the general tone is one of gloom, terror, and understated violence. The story is Faulkner's best example of these forms because it contains unimaginably dark images: a decaying mansion, a corpse, a murder, a mysterious servant who disappears, and, most horrible of all, necrophilia—an erotic or sexual attraction to corpses.

First published in the April 1930 *Saturday Evening Post*, "A Rose for Emily" was reprinted in *These Thirteen* (1931), a collection of thirteen of Faulkner's stories. It was later included in his *Collected*

Stories (1950) and in the *Selected Short Stories of William Faulkner* (1961).

Most discussions of the short story center on Miss Emily Grierson, an aristocratic woman deeply admired by a community that places her on a pedestal and sees her as "a tradition, a duty"—or, as the unnamed narrator describes her, "a fallen monument." In contrast to the community's view, we realize eventually that Miss Emily is a woman who not only poisons and kills her lover, Homer Barron, but she keeps his rotting corpse in her bedroom and sleeps next to it for many years. The ending of the story emphasizes the length of time Miss Emily must have slept with her dead lover: long enough for the townspeople to find "a long strand of iron-gray hair" lying on the pillow next to "what was left of him, rotted beneath what was left of the nightshirt" and displaying a "profound and fleshless grin."

The contrast between the aristocratic woman and her unspeakable secrets forms the basis of the story. Because the Griersons "held themselves a little too high for what they really were," Miss Emily's father forbids her to date socially, or at least the community thinks so: "None of the young men were quite good enough for Miss Emily and such." She becomes so terribly desperate for human love that she murders Homer and clings to his dead body. Using her aristocratic position to cover up the murder and the necrophilia, ironically she sentences herself to total isolation from the community, embracing the dead for solace.

Although our first reaction to the short story might be one of horror or disgust, Faulkner uses two literary techniques to create a seamless whole that makes the tale too intriguing to stop reading: the suspenseful, jumbled chronology of events, and the narrator's shifting point of view, which emphasizes Miss Emily's strength of purpose, her aloofness, and her pride, and lessens the horror and the repulsion of her actions.

Faulkner's Chronology.

One way of explaining the excellence of "A Rose for Emily" is by considering its lack of chronological order. Such a dissection of the short story initially might appear to weaken it, but this approach allows us to see Faulkner's genius at work—particularly his own, unique way of telling a story. Unlike other writers of his era, such as

John Steinbeck and Ernest Hemingway, who usually narrate their stories in a strictly linear progression, Faulkner violates all chronological sequences.

Only a few specific dates are mentioned in the story, but a close reading makes it possible to assign certain sequential events. We know, for example, that Colonel Sartoris remits Miss Emily's taxes in 1894, and that he has been dead for at least ten years when she confronts the new aldermen. Likewise, we know that she dies at the age of seventy-four. Using these facts, we can build a framework on which to hang the following chronology:

Event	Section
Miss Emily is born.	IV
She and her father ride around the town in an old, elegant carriage.	II
Her father dies, and for three days she refuses to acknowledge his death.	II
Homer Barron arrives in town and begins to court Miss Emily.	III
She buys a man's silver toilet set—a mirror, brush, and comb—and men's clothing.	IV
The town relegates her to disgrace and sends for her cousins.	III
The cousins arrive, and Homer leaves town.	IV
Three days after the cousins leave, Homer returns.	IV
Miss Emily buys poison at the local drug store.	III
Homer disappears.	IV
A horrible stench envelops Miss Emily's house.	II
Four town aldermen secretly sprinkle lime on her lawn.	II
Colonel Sartoris, the mayor, remits her taxes (1894).	I
She gives china painting lessons.	IV
Colonel Sartoris dies.	I
Miss Emily's hair turns iron-gray.	IV
She receives tax notices but returns them unopened.	I
Newly elected aldermen seek to collect her taxes, but she summarily dismisses them.	I
Miss Emily dies at age 74.	IV
Townspeople arrive at Miss Emily's house, and her black servant disappears.	V
The remains of Homer Barron are discovered.	V

Ironically, when we reconstruct the chronological arrangement in this linear fashion, we render Faulkner's masterpiece an injustice: Looking at the central events chronologically—Miss Emily buys poison, Homer Barron disappears suddenly, and a horrible stench surrounds the house—it is apparent why she buys the poison, and what causes the stench. The only surprise would be the shocking realization that Miss Emily has slept for many years in the same bed with her dead lover's rotting corpse. The horror of this knowledge makes the murder almost insignificant when compared to the necrophilia. However, the greatness of the story lies not in linearly recounting the events, but, instead, in the manner that Faulkner tells it; he leaves us horrified as we discover, bit by bit, why this so-called noble woman is now a "fallen monument."

In contrast to a traditional narrative approach, the story, as Faulkner presents it, begins with Miss Emily's funeral and ends shortly thereafter with the discovery of Homer's decayed corpse. Among other themes, it emphasizes the differences between the past, with its aristocracy—Colonel Sartoris' gallantry, the Griersons' aloofness and pride, and the board of old aldermen's respect for Miss Emily—and the modern generation's business-like mentality, embodied in the board of new aldermen and the many modern conveniences we hear about.

Section I. The story's opening lines announce the funeral of Miss Emily, to be held in her home—not in a church—and the reasons for the entire town's attending—the men out of respect for a Southern lady, the women to snoop inside her house. Her death symbolizes the passing of a genteel way of life, which is replaced by a new generation's crass way of doing things. The narrator's description of the Grierson house reinforces the disparity between the past and the present: Once a place of splendor, now modern encroachments—gas pumps and cotton wagons—obliterate most of the neighborhood and leave untouched only Miss Emily's house, with its "stubborn and coquettish decay."

This clash between the past and the present is evidenced by the different approaches that each generation takes concerning Miss Emily's taxes. In the past, Colonel Sartoris had remitted them for her, believing it uncivilized to remind a Southern woman to pay taxes, which Miss Emily does not do after her father dies. But the next generation, with its more modern ideas, holds her responsible for them. Miss Emily, however, returns the tax notice that the new aldermen send to her; when the young men call upon her, she vanquishes them, saying, "I have no taxes in Jefferson" and "See Colonel Sartoris," who has been dead for at least ten years.

One of the most striking contrasts presented in this first section entails the narrator's portrayal of Miss Emily's physical appearance and her house. Descriptive phrases include terms that add to the gothic quality of the story: She is dressed in black and leans on a cane; her "skeleton" is small; and she looks "bloated," with a "pallid hue." But Faulkner doesn't say outright that she looks much like a dead person, for it is only in retrospect that we realize that the dead-looking Miss Emily has been sleeping with the very dead Homer Barron.

Miss Emily's decaying appearance matches not only the rotting exterior of the house, but the interior as well. For example, the crayon, pastel, picture mentioned prior to the narrator's description of Miss Emily is supported by a "tarnished" stand, and Miss Emily supports herself by leaning on the "tarnished" handle of her cane. Also note that the picture is a colored chalk portrait of her father, no doubt drawn by her when she was a child. Miss Emily has *some* artistic talent: She teaches china painting, which is highly detailed and usually done in soft colors. But if she painted her father's portrait using the same techniques she uses to paint china, then the portrait would not be an accurate representation of the fiercely authoritarian man who was Mr. Grierson. It would be washed out, pale as death, a shadow of his real self.

Section II.   We return to the past, two years after Miss Emily's father's death. There have been complaints about an awful stench emanating from Miss Emily's house. The older generation, which feels that it is improper to tell a lady that she stinks, arranges for a group of men to spread lime on her lawn and inside the cellar door of her house. All the while, she sits at a window, motionless.

Of primary importance in this section is Miss Emily's relationship to her father and her reaction to his death. The town views the father and daughter as a "tableau," in which a sitting Mr. Grierson grasps a horsewhip and affects an oblivious attitude toward his daughter, who, dressed completely in white, stands behind him. This image reinforces the physical relationship and the emotional distance we feel between the two, and it recalls the crayon picture standing before the fireplace. Also, the horsewhip that Mr. Grierson clutches suggests a bridled violence in this most gothic of tales, a violence that will reveal itself by the end of the story.

When her father dies, Miss Emily cannot face the reality of his death and her loneliness. Because she has no one to turn to—"We remembered all the young men her father had driven away . . . "— for three days she insists that her father is not dead. Her clinging to him after his death prepares us for her clinging to Homer Barron after she poisons him, and we feel that her father ultimately has some responsibility for his daughter's killing her lover.

Section III. During the summer after Mr. Grierson's death, Homer Barron, a happy-go-lucky type who "was not a marrying man," and his construction crew begin to pave the town's sidewalks. Soon the townspeople begin to see Miss Emily and Homer often riding together in a buggy. At first, they acknowledge her right to date him, but they also believe that she would never consider him seriously—after all, he is "a Northerner, a day laborer," and she is a Grierson. Then the townspeople relegate her to adultery, condemning her as "fallen," and we recall the first sentence of the story, when the men of the town go to Miss Emily's funeral to pay their last respects to "a fallen monument."

A year later, Miss Emily, now over thirty, enters the town's drugstore and announces, "I want some poison." When the druggist is reluctant to sell her any without a reason, she uses her aristocratic bearing to intimidate him: "Miss Emily just stared at him, her head tilted back in order to look him eye to eye, until he looked away and went and got the arsenic and wrapped it up." At this point, we have no idea why she wants the poison, although it will become clear later that she uses the arsenic to kill Homer Barron.

Section IV. The townspeople, never suspecting that the poison is intended for Homer, conclude that Miss Emily will likely use it to kill herself. After Homer announces to the men that he is not the marrying kind, the townspeople think that his and Miss Emily's relationship is a disgrace, and they try to stop it. When they can't put an end to the relationship between the perceived lovers, they write to Miss Emily's relatives in Alabama, and two cousins come to stay with her. The town then learns that Miss Emily has bought a man's toilet set—a mirror, brush, and comb—inscribed with the initials "H.B.," and also men's clothing, including a nightshirt, which, ironically, will serve not as a *nuptial* nightshirt, but as a *burial* nightshirt for decades.

Homer disappears after Miss Emily's cousins move into the house, and everyone assumes that he has gone to prepare for Miss Emily's joining him. A week later, the cousins leave. Three days later, Homer returns. The narrator notes, "And that was the last we saw of Homer Barron." The townspeople never suspect the horror of what happens, believing that such an aristocratic woman as Miss Emily could never do any wrong. She secludes herself for six months, and when she next appears in public, she is fat and her hair is "pepper-and-salt iron-gray," the same color of the strand of hair that will be found on the pillow next to Homer's decayed corpse.

Years pass, and a new and more modern generation of people control the town. Miss Emily refuses to pay her taxes; she will not even allow postal numbers to be put on her house, a symbolic gesture on her part to resist what the town sees as progress. The narrator notes Miss Emily's staying power: "Thus she passed from generation to generation—dear, inescapable, impervious, tranquil, and perverse." The term "perverse" undoubtedly carries a double meaning—her perverseness both in refusing to pay taxes and to permit postal numbers on her house, and in nightly sleeping with a corpse.

Section V.   We return to the present and Miss Emily's funeral. Her black servant meets the mourners who arrive at the house, then he walks out the back door and disappears forever, apparently fully aware that Homer's decayed body is upstairs.

Even in death, Miss Emily cannot escape her father: "They held the funeral on the second day . . . with the crayon face of her father musing profoundly above the bier . . . " When the townspeople break into a locked room upstairs, they find carefully folded wedding clothes and Homer's remains. Only after their initial shock at seeing his skeletal corpse do they notice an indentation on the pillow next to him, with a long strand of iron-gray hair lying where a head once rested.

Because Faulkner presents his story in random fragments, it is not until the final sentence that the entire picture of Miss Emily is complete. We realize that, having been denied male companionship by her father, she is desperate for human love, so desperate that she commits murder and then uses her aristocratic position to cover up that murder. But by killing Homer, she sentences herself to total isolation. With no possibility of contact with the living, she turns to the dead.

The Narrator's Point of View.

"A Rose for Emily" is a successful story not only because of its intricately complex chronology, but also because of its unique narrative point of view. Most critics incorrectly consider the narrator, who uses "we" as though speaking for the entire town, to be young, impressionable, and male; however, on close examination, we realize that the narrator is not young and is never identified as being either male or female. The character of the narrator is better understood by examining the tone of the lines spoken by this "we" person, who changes his/her mind about Miss Emily at certain points in the narration.

Consider the opening sentence of the story and the reasons given for the townspeople's attending Miss Emily's funeral: " . . . the men [went] through a sort of respectful affection for a fallen monument." Is the narrator saying that the town views Miss Emily respectfully? Do the men remember her with affection? What has Miss Emily done to deserve the honor of being referred to as a "monument"? Once we discover that she has poisoned her lover and then slept with his dead body for an untold number of years, we wonder how the narrator can still feel affection for her. And why does the narrator think that it is important to tell us Miss Emily's story?

In general, the narrator is sympathetic to Miss Emily, never condemning her actions. Sometimes unabashedly and sometimes grudgingly, the narrator admires her ability to use her aristocratic bearing in order to vanquish the members of the city council or to buy poison. The narrator also admires her aristocratic aloofness, especially in her disdain of such common matters as paying taxes or associating with lower-class people. And yet, for a lover she chooses Homer Barron, a man of the lowest class, and more troubling than his social status is the fact that he is a Yankee. Ironically, the narrator admires Miss Emily's high-and-mighty bearing as she distances herself from the gross, vulgar, and teeming world, even while committing one of the ultimate acts of desperation—necrophilia—with a low-life Yankee.

The narrator, who does not condemn Miss Emily for her obsession with Homer, nevertheless complains that the Griersons "held themselves a little too high." But even this criticism is softened: Recalling when Miss Emily and her father rode through the town in an aristocratically disdainful manner, the narrator grudgingly admits, "We had long thought of them as a tableau"—that is, as an artistic work too refined for the common, workaday world. Also, the narrator almost perversely delights in the fact that, at age thirty, Miss Emily is still single: "We were not pleased exactly, but vindicated." After Miss Emily's father's death, the narrator's ambiguous feelings are evident: "At last [we] could pity Miss Emily." The townspeople seem glad that she is a pauper; because of her new economic status, she becomes "humanized."

Moving from admiring Miss Emily as a monument to taking petty delight in her plight, the narrator again pities her, this time when she refuses to bury her father immediately after he dies: "We remembered all the young men her father had driven away, and we knew that with nothing left, she would have to cling to that which had robbed her, as people will." The word "cling" prepares us for her clinging to Homer's dead body.

With the appearance of Homer, the narrator, now obviously representing the town's views, is "glad" that Miss Emily has a love interest, but this feeling quickly turns to indignation at the very idea of a Northerner presuming to be an equal of Miss Emily, a Southern, aristocratic lady. The narrator cannot imagine that she would stoop so low as "to forget *noblesse oblige*" and become seriously involved with a common Yankee day laborer. In other words, Miss Emily should be courteous and kind to Homer, but she should not become sexually active with him.

Once the town believes that Miss Emily is engaging in adultery, the narrator's attitude about her and Homer's affair changes from that of the town's. With great pride, the narrator asserts that Miss Emily "carried her head high enough—even when we believed that she was fallen." Unlike the town, the narrator is proud to recognize the dignity with which she faces adversity. To hold one's head high, to confront disaster with dignity, to rise above the common masses, these are the attitudes of the traditional Southern aristocracy. For example, when Miss Emily requests poison from the druggist, she does so with the same aristocratic haughtiness with which she earlier vanquished the aldermen. When the druggist asks why she wants poison, she merely stares at him, "her head tilted back in order to look him eye for eye," until he wraps up the poison for her. In the Southern culture of the time, to inquire about a person's intent was a vulgar intrusion into one's privacy. Yet, at this point, despite the narrator's admiration of Miss Emily's aristocratic haughtiness, we question a society that allows its members to use their high positions, respect, and authority to sidestep the law. We wonder about the values of the narrator.

Who, then, is this narrator, who seemingly speaks for the town but simultaneously draws back from it? The narrator makes judgments both for and against Miss Emily, and also presents outside observations—particularly in section IV, when we first learn many details about her. At the beginning of the story, the narrator seems young, is easily influenced, and is very impressed by Miss Emily's arrogant, aristocratic existence; later, in section IV, this person seems as old as Miss Emily and has related all of the important things Miss Emily has done during her lifetime; and by the story's end, the narrator, having grown old with her, is presenting her with a "rose" by sympathetically and compassionately telling her bizarre and macabre story.

By using the "we" narrator, Faulkner creates a sense of closeness between readers and his story. The narrator-as-the-town judges Miss Emily as a fallen monument, but simultaneously as a lady who is above reproach, who is too good for the common townspeople, and who holds herself aloof. While the narrator obviously admires her tremendously—the use of the word "Grierson" evokes a certain type of aristocratic behavior—the townspeople resent her arrogance and her superiority; longing to place her on a pedestal above everyone else, at the same time they wish to see her dragged down in disgrace. Nevertheless, the town, including the new council members, shows complete deference and subservience toward her. She belongs to the Old South aristocracy, and, consequently, she has special privileges.

(Here and in the following discussions, difficult words and phrases are explained.)

- **cupolas**   small, domed structures on roofs.

- **spires**   structures that taper to a point at the top; pinnacles.

- **perpetuity**   for an indefinite amount of time; forever.

- **aldermen**   members of a local legislative body; city council members.

- **gilt easel**   a gold, upright frame, or tripod, usually used to display a painting—in this case, Miss Emily's crayon picture of her father.

- **crayons**   Sticks of colored chalk, or pastels, were called crayons in this era.

- **invisible watch**   Miss Emily's watch is described as "vanishing into her waist"; symbolically, time has vanished for Miss Emily.

- **diffident deprecation**   timid disapproval.

- **lime**   Also called quicklime, this white and odorless substance has many uses, including masking foul odors.

- **tableaux**   a living representation of stock photographs of the era; however, in those photographs, the virginal-looking young woman in the background was usually a new bride, and the authoritarian man was usually a grim husband.

- **spraddled**   straddled, or sprawled.

- *noblesse oblige*   honorable behavior, considered to be the responsibility of persons of high birth or rank, to members of the lower class.

- **rustling of craned silk and satin**   The reference is to women in high-necked silk and satin dresses, "craning" their necks to spy on Miss Emily and Homer Barron.

- **Elks' Club**   a social organization that supports a variety of youth activities; persons who apply for membership must be U.S. citizens and must be sponsored by an Elks' Club member.

- **jalousies**   blinds or shutters that have adjustable horizontal slats; today, similar fixtures are known as mini-blinds.

- **a man's toilet set**   a mirror, brush, and comb.

- **cabal**   a secret group.

- **bier**   a stand on which a coffin is placed before burial.

- **sibilant voices**   conversations containing hissing sounds, such as voicing many words with the letter "s."

- **valance curtains**   ornamental drapery hung across the top edges of windows.

"THAT EVENING SUN"

"That Evening Sun" first appeared in the March 1931 issue of *American Mercury*. The remainder of its publishing history is identical to "A Rose for Emily": reprinted in *These Thirteen* (1931); in Faulkner's *Collected Stories* (1950); and in the *Selected Short Stories of William Faulkner* (1961). For anyone reading Faulkner's *The Sound and the Fury*, "That Evening Sun" provides an excellent introduction to the novel: Every character in it retains the same characteristics they have in the longer work.

The title of "That Evening Sun" refers to a popular black spiritual that begins, "Lordy, how I hate to see that evening sun go down," which implies that once the sun sets, death is sure to follow. Thus, at the end of Faulkner's short story, although some characters are not convinced that Nancy's husband, Jesus, is waiting outside her cabin to kill her, we suspect that he is close by, and that he will likely slit Nancy's throat with his razor before the night is over. The setting sun is feared by the singer of the spiritual and Nancy alike.

Many critics refer to "That Evening Sun" as one of the finest examples of narrative point of view. The story is told by Quentin Compson, whose voice Faulkner utilizes at two distinct times in the boy's life. First, we have twenty-four-year-old Quentin remembering a fifteen-year-old episode concerning Nancy's fear of Jesus. This introductory point of view is then followed by the narrative voice of nine-year-old Quentin, who recalls the episode as he experienced it at that time. Within this narration, we have the emotionally contrasting adult voices of Nancy and Mr. Compson, Quentin's father.

Because Quentin presents the story's details as he experienced them when he was nine years old, his impressions are those of a child. Limited by his young age, his perceptions of Nancy's troubling circumstances reach horrendous significance at the end of the story, when he finally understands enough to know that Jesus is probably going to kill Nancy. His main concern, however, is not with Nancy's fate; rather, he is more anxious about his own personal welfare, worrying over such a mundane problem as who will do the family's laundry after her death. His selfishness indicates his acceptance of her death as insignificant. Likewise, he and his sister, Caddy, and their younger brother, Jason, do not understand the significance of most of the story's events, including why Nancy gets several of her teeth knocked out by Mr. Stovall, the Baptist deacon; why Nancy tries to hang herself; and what the "watermelon" is under her dress. Most important, the children will never comprehend the abject horror that she suffers.

The dual points of view are best illustrated by Faulkner's brilliantly contrasting Nancy's and the Compson children's fears. Nancy's sense of impending doom and her debilitating fear in the face of her imminent death are strikingly dissimilar to the Compson children's playing their games of "scary cat." Nancy is terrified by premonitions of her rapidly approaching death, whereas the children try to frighten each other by using such insignificant things as darkness.

Faulkner uses these disparate voices to weave themes that contribute to the story's richness. Included in these themes is the implied dissolution of Southern aristocracy. The Compson family is on a personal and social decline that loosely parallels Nancy's decline. Mr. Compson is cold and detached; Mrs. Compson is whining and neurotic; nine-year-old Quentin is calm and rational; seven-year-old Caddy is inquisitive and daring; and five-year-old Jason is unpleasant and obnoxious. As is always true of Faulkner, we have the distinction between the rich and the poor, and, more important, the inequality and the prejudice found in the treatment of blacks by their white counterparts. For example, Nancy is often a sexual object for some of the town's white men, and she assumes that the child she is carrying has a white father. We hear that her husband, Jesus, is not allowed to come even to the back doors or kitchens of white houses, to which he remarks, "But white man can hang around mine. White man can come in my house, but I cant stop him. When white man want to come in my house, I aint got no house." Such is the prejudicial double standard that still existed at the time of Faulkner's writing this short story.

Section I. The opening of "That Evening Sun" emphasizes the differences between the past and the present, much like the opening section of "A Rose for Emily." Quentin is twenty-four years old, and laundry is now delivered in automobiles. There are electric line poles and paved streets; even the black women who still take in laundry have their husbands pick it up and deliver it in cars. But fifteen years earlier, the streets would have been filled with black women carrying bundles of clothes balanced on their heads. Nancy was one of the women whom the Compson children liked to watch carry laundry on her head because she could balance her bundle while crawling through fences or walking down in ditches and then up out of them. Sometimes, the husbands of the washing women would fetch and deliver the clothes for their wives, but Jesus, Nancy's husband, would never stoop to this servitude for her.

The emphasis on washing both in the first and last sections unifies the story. The opening paragraphs describe the children's interest in Nancy as a washerwoman; the story ends with Quentin's accepting Nancy's death and wondering, "Who will do our washing now, Father?" Likewise, the opening emphasizes how Jesus is different from other husbands; at the end, he is likely outside Nancy's shack, waiting to kill her.

This first section provides much background information. When Dilsey, the Compsons' cook, is sick, Nancy has to cook for the family, and the children, always thinking that she is drunk, have to go to her cabin to wake her. However, when Nancy is arrested, the children come to believe that her problem isn't alcohol, but drugs. On the way to jail, Nancy passes Mr. Stovall, a deacon in the Baptist church, and she begins to plead with the white man: "When you going to pay me, white man? It's been three times now since you paid me a cent—" The Baptist deacon knocks her down and kicks out several of her teeth, and Nancy is taken to jail. There, she tries to hang herself by removing her dress and using it as a noose. The jailer reports that it is not whiskey that is the cause of Nancy's problems; rather, it is cocaine, because "no nigger would try to commit suicide unless he was full of cocaine, because a nigger full of cocaine wasn't a nigger any longer."

Several of Nancy's teeth are kicked out because of a Southern racial distinction that allows a white Baptist deacon, such as Mr. Stovall, to use Nancy as a sexual object, regardless of whether he pays her or not. But a black man could be hanged immediately if he even spoke familiarly with a white woman. Mr. Stovall, of course, knows that he will not be punished for striking Nancy. At the time the story takes place, a white man could harm a black person without the least fear of recrimination.

This episode also highlights the theme of small-town mentality. Quentin reports the encounter between Nancy and Mr. Stovall, but he himself didn't witness it. Instead, he knows about the incident because it soon becomes the talk of the town: "That was how she lost her teeth, and all that day they told about Nancy and Mr. Stovall, and all that night the ones that passed the jail could hear Nancy singing and yelling." In a small town, this event would provide a great deal of gossipy enjoyment.

Pregnant likely with a white man's child, Nancy attempts suicide; the jailer finds her "hanging from the window, stark naked, her belly already swelling out a little, like a little balloon." This suggestion of her being pregnant leads Quentin to recall a conversation between Nancy and Jesus. He and his siblings overheard them talking about Nancy's swelling under her apron, and Jesus said that it was a "watermelon." When Nancy retorted, "It never come off your vine, though," Jesus responded, with a hint of future violence, "I can cut down the vine it did come off of." Quentin merely reports these sexually charged innuendoes, including his sister Caddy's questioning the two adults about their statements. Again, we have a double vision: The adults discuss a subject that belongs to the adult world, and the young listeners misunderstand the sexual nature of that discussion.

So far, Faulkner has presented only background information. At this point, the main plot, narrated by nine-year-old Quentin, begins with his announcing that Nancy has finished washing the supper dishes, but that she remains sitting in the kitchen. After speaking to Nancy, Mr. Compson tells his wife that he is going to escort Nancy home because she fears that Jesus is back in town. She is afraid that he will kill her for being pregnant with someone else's child— especially, a white man's. Mrs. Compson accuses her husband of being more concerned with Nancy's safety than with her own. Her objection is a ridiculous complaint: In the Southern culture in which she lives, no black person, not even the feared Jesus, would break into the Compson mansion or threaten Mrs. Compson.

The children quickly decide to go with Nancy and their father. Nancy explains that Jesus was always good to her, but now nobody can protect her from his wrath. Listening to Mr. Compson tell her that this would never have happened if she had "let white men alone," Nancy is adamant that Jesus is close by. She can feel him, and she knows that she will see him only one more time, immediately before he cuts her throat with a razor. Mr. Compson tries to assure her that Jesus is most likely in St. Louis with another woman by now, to which she responds that if she ever finds out that Jesus is cheating on her, she will cut off his head and slit the woman's belly. Her response is ironic given that this murderous violence is exactly what Nancy fears from Jesus.

However, we should be aware that, essentially, Nancy is not blaming Jesus for wanting to kill her. Because she would decapitate Jesus for fooling around, she knows that Jesus is justified in using a razor on her for cheating on him. Nevertheless, she fears having her throat cut, all alone, in the darkening night.

The children are ignorant of and unconcerned about Nancy's mounting anxieties. Walking to her cabin, they prattle constantly about which one of them is more scared. Caddy begins to tease Jason that he is a "scairy cat," which he fervently denies. By teasing each other, the children are clearly unaware of the abject terror that Nancy is feeling. None of them—particularly the inquisitive Caddy—understands the crux of Nancy and Mr. Compson's conversation. For example, when Mr. Compson tells Nancy that Jesus would not be upset if only Nancy had "let white men alone," Caddy immediately wants to know, "Let what white men alone? . . . How let them alone?" Later, when Nancy threatens to slit the belly of whichever woman Jesus is with, Caddy again wants to know, "Slit whose belly, Nancy?" Although Quentin never joins in the teasing between Caddy and Jason, his narrating their childish play without commenting on how inappropriate it is, given Nancy's predicament, suggests that even Quentin sees nothing wrong with his siblings' banter. He is a child relating what he sees and hears.

Nancy does not feel in control of her own fate. She constantly reiterates, "I aint nothing but a nigger. . . . It aint none of my fault." This response is not surprising when we consider that the Southern aristocratic society castigated blacks as worthless. Nancy has internalized this condemnation to so great an extent that she believes her life is without value.

Section II. Because Dilsey remains sick, Nancy continues to cook for the family. Mr. Compson and the children walk her home every night, until Mrs. Compson complains, "How much longer is this going on? I to be left alone in this big house while you take home a frightened Negro?" Her nagging takes its toll on her husband, for he eventually makes a pallet for Nancy in the kitchen, where she can sleep. One night, after the family awakes to a sound coming from the kitchen, Mr. Compson goes downstairs to check on the noise and returns with Nancy and the pallet, which he puts in Quentin and Caddy's bedroom.

This episode is important thematically and contains one of the clues that convinces many readers that Nancy is murdered at the story's end. Obviously having heard something outside the house and believing it is Jesus, she begins panicking. Although the children cannot describe exactly the agitated sound that Nancy makes, Faulkner characterizes the children's impression of it in words that he repeats in the final section of the story. Here in this section, Quentin notes of Nancy's moaning, "It was not singing and it was not crying, coming up the dark stairs. . . . It was like singing and it wasn't like singing, like the sounds that Negroes make." This description is similar to that in the last section, when Mr. Compson and the children leave Nancy in her shack, waiting for Jesus. Although they cannot see her, they can hear her: " . . . she began just after we came up out of the ditch, the sound that was not singing and not unsinging." This sound that Nancy makes in the final section recalls the sound from section II and alerts us that she must hear Jesus outside, waiting to kill her.

Also significant in the pallet scene is Quentin's beginning to understand subtle nuances in how adults act and what they say. Lying on the pallet, Nancy whispers in a frightened tone, "Jesus." Quentin describes Nancy's saying the word as "Jeeeeeeeeeeeeeeee-sus," to which Caddy inquisitively asks, "Was it Jesus?" Understanding that Nancy does not mean her husband, but Jesus Christ, Quentin comments to his sister, "It's the other Jesus she means." He is acquiring the ability to differentiate between Nancy's fear of her husband and her call for her savior's protection.

Again, Nancy disclaims any self-worth. Ironically, although she calls to her savior, she then speaks of God's knowing that "I aint nothing but a nigger." Because she has been so conditioned by the Southern culture to believe that she is worthless, she thinks God believes this, too.

When Dilsey returns to the Compson household, she resumes the cooking; that night, Nancy arrives, saying she knows that Jesus is outside, waiting to kill her. The conversation between her and Dilsey continues the theme of the Compson children's lack of concern for her situation. Jason's interjections are similar to his and

Caddy's sparring in section I about whether or not he is a "scairy cat." In this section, his concern about who is a "nigger" contrasts with the seriousness of Nancy and Dilsey's discussion and reinforces our impression that Jason is a mouthy, overly pampered brat.

Nancy's final remarks at the end of this section—"I wont be nothing soon. I going back where I come from soon"—accentuate the intense fear and self-loathing that she continues to feel. The tension mounts as no one—except us—sympathizes with her plight.

Section III.   Nancy tries to drink some coffee, but she is so terrified of her husband and his razor that she cannot swallow. When she tells Dilsey, "Wont no nigger stop him," Dilsey agrees, which is the first personal acknowledgment that Nancy's fears are justified. Mr. Compson appears to recognize Nancy's fears, but because of his wife, he is trapped as to how much he can help her. For example, he would allow Nancy to continue to sleep in the Compson house, but Mrs. Compson, selfish and bigoted, says, "I cant have Negroes sleeping in the bedrooms."

The Compsons' conversation, besides reaffirming Mrs. Compson's bigotry, juxtaposes again the adults' and children's worlds. When Mrs. Compson wonders why the law cannot do anything to stop Jesus, Caddy asks, "Are you afraid of father, mother?" Acting like a child herself, Mrs. Compson fails to understand Nancy's fear, nor can she comprehend being left alone again while Mr. Compson escorts Nancy home. In the single instance in which Mr. Compson stands up for Nancy, he tells his wife dryly, "You know that I am not lying outside with a razor."

Nancy's fear and anxiety are so great that she cannot even hold a cup, and deep, rumbling noises emanate from her body. Again, she makes sounds that foreshadow those she will make in the last section of the story, and Faulkner uses the same phrases that he does at the end of the story to characterize these sounds: "She began to make the sound again, not loud. Not singing and not unsinging."

Not wanting to walk home alone, Nancy begs the children to accompany her, but she cannot convince Jason to go with her. Caddy maintains that Jason is too scared and will tell their parents. Ironically, he agrees to go simply because of his sister's accusations. As they walk to the cabin, Nancy talks to the children in a very loud voice, hoping that if Jesus is close by, he will think that Mr. Compson is with them. Caddy cannot understand why Nancy speaks so loudly, nor why she calls Jason "Mr. Jason," the name of their father.

Once at her cabin, Nancy is absolutely frantic to keep the children's attention, knowing that the second their interest wanes, they will want to go back home. Quentin observes that when Nancy tells a story to the children, "She talked like her eyes looked, like her eyes watching us and her voice talking to us did not belong to her. Like she was living somewhere else, waiting somewhere else." Projecting herself into the story of a queen who comes up out of a ditch to get to her cabin to bar the door, which she and the children have just done, Nancy cannot separate her own fears from the story's narration.

Section IV. After Nancy fails to hold the children's attention, she becomes obsessed to keep them with her. She believes their presence will keep her from death, or at least prolong its inevitability. So completely terrified that she does not even notice that her hand rests on a hot lamp globe, her fear makes her impervious to physical pain, and her emotional stability is strained by Jason's constant crying to go home.

Nothing seems to work for her. The popcorn popper breaks, but once she fixes it, the popcorn will not pop. The normality that she so desperately craves is interrupted by a smoking lamp, which she has turned up too high, hoping that the strong light will keep Jesus away. When the popcorn popper falls in the fire and Jason gets smoke in his eyes and begins to cry, Nancy realizes that the end is near. Breaking out in a profuse sweat, she pleads with the children to stay or to let her come with them back to their house.

She becomes almost hysterical as she senses her impending doom. Physically, "sitting there above the fire, her long hands dangling between her knees," she gives up all hope of fighting off what she now considers inevitable. Quentin notes that she is an emotional wreck: "Then Nancy began to make that sound again, not loud . . . "

Section V. Mr. Compson, who has come to take the children back home, refuses to believe that Jesus is outside, but Nancy explains that he has left a sign—"a hogbone, with blood meat on it"—to warn her that he will kill her. She tells Mr. Compson, "When yawl walk out that door, I gone." Continuing the adult-child theme of understanding the world, Caddy takes this statement literally and wants to know, "Gone where, Nancy?" Jason's response to the situation is characteristic of what we have come to expect of him: He is concerned only that he not be branded a tattletale.

Nancy, knowing that it will do no good to try to escape her fate, rejects Mr. Compson's offer to take her to Aunt Rachel's. She accepts that, because she had sex with white men, she will get what is her due: "I reckon it belong to me. I reckon what I going to get ain't no more than mine." By her own standards—she threatened to kill Jesus for cheating on her—Jesus has the right to kill her, but the horror and the fear are still overwhelmingly intense.

Mr. Compson wants Nancy to bar the door and turn off the light, but she is frightened of being killed in the dark. Ironically, like little Jason, she, too, is afraid of the dark: "I scared for it to happen in the dark." She reminds them that as soon as they leave, "I gone," but she is somewhat resigned to her death, taking consolation in the fact that her coffin is already paid for.

Section VI. As the Compson family leaves the resigned but terrified Nancy, they look back through the shack's open door and see her sitting before the fire. Then, as they cross the ditch, they can't see her anymore, yet her door is still open and the fire is still burning. Quentin recalls Nancy's phrase, "I just done got tired. . . . I just a nigger. It ain't no fault of mine." She has accepted the position assigned to her by both white and black society and sits waiting for her death.

Caddy, who still has no clue about Nancy's imminent death, asks her father, "What's going to happen?" It is Quentin who makes the most telling statement: He wonders aloud, "Who will do our washing now, Father?" Blandly accepting Nancy's premise that she will be killed that night, his main concern is not with her death, but with who will do the family's washing.

The magnificent closing features Caddy and Jason bickering, with Caddy teasing Jason about how scared of the dark he would be if the others weren't with him. The story ends not with the bang of Nancy's death, which is symbolized by "the sound that was not singing and not unsinging," but with the whimper of two small children and the futile shout of their ineffective father.

- **iron poles bearing clusters of bloated and ghostly and bloodless grapes** In this image, referring to electrical poles with clusters of clear glass insulators that protect electrical wires, Faulkner draws attention to the sterility of the story's Southern culture.

- **deacon** a layperson who assists the minister of a church.

- **pallet** A term predominantly used in the Southern states, a pallet is made of several layers of sheets, blankets, or quilts, folded over and then laid on the floor.

- **coffin money** At the time that "That Evening Sun" takes place, few blacks could afford insurance, except for what was called "burial insurance." As explained in the story, an agent collected fifteen cents every week—$7.80 per year—from a person to be used for burial expenses. Because of the high cost of coffins, people could never pay their total bill in full, and therefore they might pay fifteen cents per week for their entire lives. This practice was another way the white Southern culture kept blacks in desperate circumstances.

"BARN BURNING"

Faulkner's short story about Sarty Snopes and his father, Abner Snopes, has been praised ever since its first publication in *Harper's Magazine* for June 1939. It was reprinted in his *Collected Stories* (1950) and in the *Selected Short Stories of William Faulkner* (1961). Part of the story's greatness is due to its major theme, the conflict between loyalty to one's family and loyalty to honor and justice. This conflict is vividly illustrated by having a young ten-year-old boy—Sarty—confront this dilemma as part of his initiation into manhood.

Young Sarty has a choice: He can be loyal to his father, his blood relative, or he can do what he innately senses is right. He knows that his father is wrong when he burns barns, but Abner constantly reminds his son of the importance of family blood, and of the responsibilities that being part of a family entails. He tells Sarty, "You got to learn to stick to your own blood or you ain't going to have any blood to stick to you." In other words, if you are not utterly loyal to your own family, no matter if the family is right or wrong, then you will have no place to turn when you need help. At the end of the story, this is Sarty's dilemma—he has no place to go and no one to turn to.

The opening of "Barn Burning" emphasizes the antithetical loyalties that confront Sarty. The setting is a makeshift court for a Justice of the Peace, for Abner Snopes has been accused of burning Mr. Harris' barn. Immediately, Sarty is convinced that the people in the court are his and his father's enemies. He fiercely aligns himself with a loyalty to blood and kin, as opposed to the justice of the court: " . . . *our enemy* he thought in that despair; *ourn! Mine and hisn both!*

He's my father!" Faulkner then recounts the events that have led up to the charge against Sarty's father: Mr. Harris had warned Snopes to keep his hog out of the farmer's cornfield, and he had even given Snopes enough wire to pen the hog; after the hog escaped yet again into Harris' field, the farmer kept the hog and charged Snopes a dollar for "pound fee"; Snopes paid the fee and sent word to Harris that "wood and hay kin burn." Because there is no proof—other than this enigmatic message—that Snopes is responsible for burning the barn, the judge is legally forced to find him innocent. However, he warns Snopes to leave the county and not come back.

The courtroom scene and the following fight outside between Sarty and some boys underscore Sarty's predicament. Called to testify during the hearing, he is about to confess his father's guilt when the judge dismisses him; yet, when he is outside the courtroom and hears the boys calling his father a barn burner, he comes immediately to his father's defense, engaging them in a fight during which he sheds his own blood to protect his father's—and his own—name. Thus, the literal importance of blood loyalty is strongly emphasized.

These opening scenes provide us with a clear picture of Abner Snopes, whose last name itself—beginning with the "sn" sound—is unpleasant sounding. A silent and sullen man, he walks with a limp, a significant factor when we learn later that he received the wound while stealing horses—and not necessarily the enemy's—during the Civil War. We also discover that Harris' barn is not the first barn that he has burned.

Snopes never burns farm houses, and while we might initially conclude that this restraint is proof that Snopes isn't wholly incorrigible, we soon learn that on farms, barns are more important than houses because they hold livestock and oftentimes harvested crops, which provide the money and food that farmers and their families need to survive. Farms can thrive without houses, but they are doomed to fail without barns. Abner, of course, is keenly aware of this fact.

Although he knows that his father is a barn burner, Sarty fights the boys to defend his father's integrity, while hoping fervently that his father will stop burning barns: *"Forever* he thought. *Maybe he's done satisfied now, now that he has . . . "* Sarty cannot complete his thought that his father is not only a barn burner, but that he has been one for so long that before he burns down one barn, he has "already arranged to make a crop on another farm before he . . . " Again, Sarty severs his thought before he comes to the logical conclusion. He cannot bring himself to finish the sentence, which presumably would end, "before he . . . burnt down the barn."

Following the courtroom scene, Snopes loads his family into a wagon, headed for another farm on which to work. That night at a makeshift camp, he calls for Sarty to join him in a walk, and their ensuing conversation elaborates again the theme of family loyalty versus truth and justice. Realizing that Sarty was going to tell the Justice of the Peace the truth about the barn burning, Abner slaps his son in a dispassionate manner, much like he earlier whipped the mules that pulled the wagon—"without heat." He warns Sarty about the importance of family and explains that none of the men in the courtroom would have defended *him*. Fearful of his father's abusive behavior, Sarty knows that it is useless to respond: "If I had said they wanted only truth, justice, he would have hit me again."

The campfire episode is also important because it affords Faulkner the opportunity to explain to us why Snopes burns barns. Faulkner notes that the campfire is small, and he contemplates why Abner, who has such a penchant for fire, doesn't build a larger one. Explaining that an older Sarty might also wonder why, he provides two possible reasons: Because Abner was always hiding from troops during the Civil War, he grew accustomed to building small fires, which would not expose his location; but Faulkner settles on a better explanation, that fire "spoke to some deep mainspring" of Abner's character "as the one weapon for the preservation of integrity . . . and hence to be regarded with respect and used with discretion." The threat of fire is his one and only source of power, to be used selectively and effectively should anyone cross his path and anger him.

When the family arrives at the new sharecropping farm, Snopes takes Sarty along with him to see Major de Spain, "the man that aims to begin to-morrow owning me body and soul for the next eight months." Arriving at the landowner's mansion, Sarty is astonished by its size. Faulkner emphasizes his theme of justice by having Sarty compare the de Spain mansion to a place of law: "Hit's big as a courthouse . . . They are safe from him." Sarty thinks that the mere magnificence of the mansion will stop his father from burning more barns. This belief, no matter how false it might be, creates "a surge of peace and joy" within the young boy, who has known only a life of "frantic grief and despair." He hopes that his father will be as affected by the house's grandeur as he is, and that the stateliness of de Spain's plantation will "even change him now from what maybe he couldn't help but be." Sarty's dream is admirable and demonstrates his youthful innocence, but we know that he will be sorely disappointed.

Immediately, Sarty notices that his father possesses a "stiff black back" that is not dwarfed by the house. Snopes is defiant of the mansion's magnificence, and as Sarty watches him walk down the lane toward the house, we are presented with the central image of the story:

> Watching him, the boy remarked the absolutely undeviating course which his father held and saw the stiff foot come squarely down in a pile of fresh droppings where a horse had stood in the drive and which his father could have avoided by a simple change of stride.

As they approach the front of the house, the butler meets them at the door, telling Snopes to wipe his feet before entering, to which Abner responds with a command to the butler, "Get out of my way, nigger." When Mrs. de Spain orders Snopes out of the house after he deliberately tracks dung on her rug, he pivots intentionally so that his boot makes a "final long and fading smear." Leaving, he wipes the rest of the manure from his boot on the front steps before looking back at the mansion and commenting: "Pretty and white, ain't it? . . . That's sweat. Nigger sweat. Maybe it ain't white enough yet to suit him. Maybe he wants to mix some white sweat with it."

This encounter, featuring Snopes and his defilement of the de Spain mansion, is the central motivation for the story. To Sarty, the mansion represents everything associated with truth, justice, and culture. That his father could so deliberately soil the aristocratic house with horse manure is inconceivable to him. It is, however, significant that the smearing is done with Snopes' wounded foot, which suggests his evil character. We know that he was wounded in the Civil War, and because he had no allegiance to either side, he is resentful of his current place in life—a resentment that causes him to strike out blindly at any and all forces that oppose him, or that he perceives as a threat.

Snopes feels superior only when he encounters someone who is black—in this case, the butler. Except in the South, nowhere in the United States could such a white-trash character like Abner Snopes enter the front door of a mansion if the butler forbade entry. However, in the South at the time the story takes place, a black person could not deny admittance to a Southern white person. More accurately, black men could not, under any circumstances, ever touch a white man, even if that white man was not part of the Southern aristocracy. Consequently, Snopes can feel superior to the black butler only because his own skin is white.

Two hours later, Sarty sees de Spain ride up to his father. Along with Sarty, we do not know what trespasses between the two men, but it is soon apparent that de Spain has brought the rug for Snopes to clean. Later, not satisfied with the way his two "bovine" daughters do the job, Snopes picks up a field stone and begins to vigorously scrub—and ruin—the rug himself. His motivations for deliberately soiling and then ruining the rug are essentially related to his wounded foot and his wounded pride. He resents being treated worse than most blacks would be treated, and he is angered by de Spain's contempt for him.

Early the next morning, Sarty is awakened by his father, who tells him to saddle the mule. With Sarty riding and Snopes walking, they carry the rolled-up rug back to de Spain's, throw it on his front porch, and return home. Later that morning, de Spain rides up and infuriatingly tells Snopes that the rug is ruined, and that he is charging him twenty bushels of corn for destroying it, in addition to what Snopes already owes for renting the farm.

The snobbish tone that de Spain uses to berate Snopes—"But you never had a hundred dollars. You never will."—prompts Sarty to side with his father against the landowner. Sarty affectionately addresses his father as "Pap" and promises that de Spain "won't git no twenty bushels! He won't git none!" In supporting his father against de Spain, he distinguishes between the severity of burning a barn and his father's role in ruining the rug. While barn burning is intolerable to Sarty, twenty bushels of corn as punishment for destroying a rug is excessive injustice, as the Justice of the Peace will rule later. However, Sarty notes, one benefit of his father's having to pay the twenty bushels is that it might make him " . . . *stop forever and always from being what he used to be.*" Sarty's hoping for something to happen that will force his father to quit burning barns emphasizes his innate desire to conform to society's justice—so long as that justice is fair.

When Sarty discovers that his father must appear before the Justice of the Peace, he does not know that his father is the plaintiff and not the defendant. In the courtroom, he cries out to the judge, "He ain't done it! He ain't burnt . . . " before his father shuts him up. Instinctively, Sarty comes to his father's defense, which emphasizes his family loyalty, although we know that he remains upset by previous barn burnings.

After the judge rules that Snopes owes ten bushels of corn rather than twenty, Sarty, still loyal to the family, sides with his father and says that de Spain "won't git no ten bushels neither. He won't git one." Snopes tells his son, " . . . we'll wait," implying that the matter is still open to debate—de Spain does have a barn that can be burned. Although we are not aware of it until later that night, Snopes feels defeated again by the aristocracy; he feels inferior. His determination to revenge the court's decision is revealed by the simple statement he gives his son.

That night at home, we hear Sarty's mother cry out suddenly, "Abner! No! No! Oh, God. Oh, God. Abner!" Having lost his lawsuit, Snopes is preparing to set fire to de Spain's barn. After Sarty hears his mother's cry, immediately he sees a horrifying image: His father is still dressed in his black suit, "at once formal and burlesque." This same black suit that Snopes wore to the legal hearing now becomes a suit for some "shabby and ceremonial violence." The irony lies in the fact that Snopes, by his formal dress, is preparing for his ritualistic act of burning barns.

That Sarty's mother is so opposed to her husband's actions—to the point that she is brutally abused by him—foreshadows Sarty's own opposition to this senseless and violent crime. When his father orders him to get more oil, he briefly hesitates. He is faced with three options: He can go along with his father, thus becoming a co-conspirator in the crime; he can *run on and on and never look back, never need to see his face again*"; or he can try either to stop his father or warn de Spain. Sarty embraces this third option when he pleads with his father, "Ain't you going to even send a nigger? . . . At least you sent a nigger before!" We recall that in the story's initial courtroom scene, Mr. Harris claimed that a black man delivered a threatening message to him from Snopes; now, Snopes is not going to give de Spain any warning.

Before Snopes leaves the house, he instructs his wife to hold Sarty tightly, knowing that his son will warn de Spain of the impending barn burning and thwart his revenge. He now knows, with certainty, that Sarty is torn between loyalty to his family and his need to enforce principles of justice.

After his father leaves, Sarty tries to break loose from his mother; his aunt, who joins in his pleas to let him go, threatens to go herself to warn de Spain. Ultimately, we realize, the aunt, the mother, and Sarty are all on the same side—the side of justice. This fact is important to note because otherwise, we might consider Sarty an anomaly, but with his mother and aunt's agreeing with him, his role as an advocate of justice is more convincing.

As soon as he is free, Sarty runs to de Spain's, bursts into the house, and cries out, "Barn! . . . Barn!" He then flees down the road and is almost run over by de Spain on a galloping horse, headed for his barn. Sarty begins to run again, and suddenly he hears one gunshot followed by two more. He stops and yells, "Pap! Pap!"—his affectionate term for his father. Blindly running again, he falls down and calls out, "Father! Father!" There is little doubt that his father is dead.

At midnight, Sarty sits on the crest of a hill, his "grief and despair now no longer terror and fear but just grief and despair." He attempts to reassure himself that his father had been in the Civil War and had served honorably in Colonel Sartoris' cavalry. Faulkner comments that Sarty is unaware that his father went to war not out of a sense of loyalty, but for "booty—it meant nothing and less than nothing to him if it were enemy booty or his own." Later, Sarty realizes that he must have fallen asleep because it is almost dawn. He gets up and continues walking down the road.

The central image at the end of "Barn Burning" is one of rebirth and renewal, a typical image to end an initiation-into-manhood story. Sarty is headed "toward the dark woods," from which he hears birds calling. Their "liquid silver voices" symbolize the vitality of the spring morning and, by extension, the unceasing spirit of Sarty Snopes. We feel certain of his devotion to the justice that he has sought throughout the story; as Faulkner notes of him, "He did not look back."

These final images focus on Sarty: He is alone—he has cut himself off from his family and now must face the world by himself, possessing nothing but his own integrity and a strong sense of justice. He never again appears in any of Faulkner's works, although Abner Snopes and Sarty's older brother become central figures in other stories and novels. It is as though Faulkner did not want a male Snopes with a moral conscience present amidst the other amoral, unethical, thieving, and degenerate male members.

- **a dollar pound fee** A "pound" is an enclosure in which stray animals are kept. Mr. Harris charges Abner Snopes a dollar for keeping Abner's hog penned up and out of the corn.

- **provost** the head of a military police unit; Abner Snopes was shot in the heel by a member of a Confederate provost's unit, emphasizing his despicable character; he also stole horses from fellow Southerners during the Civil War.

- **portico** a porch with a roof supported by columns.

- **sorrel mare** a mare that is yellowish to reddish brown.

- **a fat bay** a reddish brown horse.

- **scoriations** derived from the word "score," which means to make grooves on a surface; Faulkner often made up words when he wrote.

- **lilliputian** Meaning very small, the word comes from Jonathan Swift's *Gulliver's Travels*, in which the Lilliputians, a race of small people, capture Gulliver.

- **hame** one of the two curved pieces that fit around a horse's neck; straps or chains are attached from the hame to the wagon to pull the vehicle.

- **logger-head** a blockhead or a dolt; Faulkner calls Snopes' mule a logger-head to emphasize the animal's stupidity.

- **a middle buster** a type of plow used to bust up the ground before planting crops; typically, a middle buster prepares a ridge for cotton, potatoes, sweet potatoes, or other crops that are planted in ridges, not furrows.

- **cravat** a scarf, or band of fabric loosely knotted around the neck like a tie.

- **tulle** a finely meshed net used for veils or gowns.

- **Malbrouck** Faulkner invented many fictitious names to add flavor to his writing—as he does with "Malbrouck."

- **booty**   stolen goods.

- **quiring**   an archaic version of choir; a reference to the earlier mention of the "liquid silver voices of the birds."

"DRY SEPTEMBER"

As a Southern writer, Faulkner draws upon the mores and prejudices of his own regional culture to create unforgettable characters and settings for his novels and short stories. "Dry September" clearly shows the horrible miscarriages of justice that prejudice can cause. Although the story revolves around the killing of Will Mayes, the actual act of killing is omitted in order to keep our attention focused on the causes of the violence, and on the mental and physical atmospheres that breed such senseless and random acts of cruelty.

First published in the January 1931 edition of *Scribner's Magazine*, "Dry September" was reprinted in Faulkner's *Collected Stories* (1950) and in the *Selected Short Stories of William Faulkner* (1961). This powerful study of a cultural mentality that promotes rash, swift killings of black men is based on the Southern White Goddess concept. To understand fully the themes and setting of the story, we need to have some knowledge of this White Goddess concept, which applies not only to "Dry September," but to any Southern story dealing with womanhood and rape, including Faulkner's *Light in August* and Harper Lee's popular *To Kill a Mockingbird*.

In its simplest form, the White Goddess concept refers to any "lily-white" Southern woman, who is raised in a society that protects her from any unpleasantries. Because she is white, the culture sets her atop a mythical pedestal, creating an imaginary, protective shield through which the Southern aristocracy lets nothing pass that might endanger—both physically and emotionally—its women. While the Southern white male will allow a woman to fib or tell "white lies" about insignificant matters, he believes adamantly that a Southern lady could never outright lie; even if she did, a Southern gentleman would never confront her with the lie. Instead, it is obligatory that the white man act upon the premise that a Southern woman can tell nothing but the truth. Psychologically, this complete deference to a woman's integrity is based on the belief that she could never be attracted to a black man; consequently, she would never lie about such a matter.

"Dry September," short though it may be, addresses many aspects of this Southern culture. Rather than emphasize the violence of Will Mayes' death, the story focuses on the causes leading up to that violence and the mentality that breeds such monstrous behavior. Closely related to this sadism is a sense of insecurity. For example, John McLendon, the leader of the murderous mob, might be skilled in killing defenseless blacks, but he is anything but successful in his private life. He physically abuses his wife, and his house is described as "a birdcage and almost as small . . . " Unable to face personal failure, he turns to various acts of sadism, whether they be against Will Mayes or his passive, mothering wife.

Faulkner treats many of his characters as victims of various societal forces. Of course, Will Mayes is the most obvious victim. The only character who evokes our complete sympathy, he does nothing to make us believe that he is guilty of raping his accuser, Miss Minnie Cooper. But Miss Minnie is also a victim, a victim of her own sexual frustration. She is driven to desperation by her "idle and empty days": She has no occupation, no social position, and no intellectual interests. Trapped by her advancing age, she fantasizes, hoping that the mere hint of rape will prove her still sexually desirable. McLendon is also somewhat of a victim—if only of the hot and arid weather—but his problem stems from an insecurity that he compensates for with violent actions. Note that every description of McLendon emphasizes his violence: His face is "furious," and his movements are described as violent and barely under his control. After striking his wife, he tears through the house "ripping off his shirt" and then hunting "furiously" for it.

The story is divided into five sections: Sections I and III show the town's reaction to the rumor that Miss Minnie, a spinster, has been attacked by Will Mayes, a black man; parts II and IV familiarize us with Miss Minnie's history and give us an inside view of her emotional state; and section V provides us with a glimpse of McLendon's home life and his rebellious tyranny over his wife.

Section I.   The opening paragraph of "Dry September" sets the tone of the story by focusing on the oppressive heat and the resultant, uncontrolled and heated passions of Jefferson's citizens. Sixty-two hot, rainless days have created a frustration among the townspeople and have fueled Miss Minnie's accusation that she was raped by a black man. The first sentence stresses the rapidity with which the rumor—"like a fire in dry grass"—has spread throughout the town. The dry spell also causes the twilight to appear "bloody red," which emphasizes the bloody events that are about to transpire. Already fueling people's need for violence, the alleged attack has occurred in the early morning of the day that begins the story. Faulkner establishes a major theme by linking the rumor of Miss Minnie's attack and the weather: Throughout the story, characters refer to the weather as an excuse for their behavior.

The first few paragraphs—typically Faulknerian with their long sentences of distorted but elaborate syntax—suggest another major theme, the questionable reliability of Miss Minnie's accusation. The men assembled in the barbershop are unsure about the Southern woman's claim: "Attacked, insulted, frightened: none of them . . . knew exactly what had happened," or whether anything had happened at all. We must remember the discussion of the White Goddess concept as we form opinions about these men; it should surprise none of us that many characters, although they have their private doubts about the truthfulness of Miss Minnie's claim, do nothing to question her or to stop the killing.

Appropriately, the story begins in a barber shop, a symbolic gathering place for small-town gossipers. The spokesman for quiet, calm justice is Henry Hawkshaw, one of the barbers. In his support of the accused Will Mayes, Hawkshaw is instantly on the defensive as he insists repeatedly that those men who want to act rashly should first find out the facts before they rush to judgment.

In the midst of the tension caused by the rumor, Hawkshaw is the voice of reason. His patience and persistence in wanting facts and justice represent the sane approach—in contrast to the others' irrational violence. But he is immediately trapped by the stereotype of being a "damn niggerlover." At the time of this story, if a Southern white person defended a black man, that person automatically was called a "niggerlover." To a white Southerner, the horror of being called this epithet far outweighed a need for any justice: When McLendon demands to know "Who's with me?" some of the men enthusiastically join him, while others "sat uncomfortable, not looking at one another, then one by one they rose and joined him." These holdouts eventually give in out of fear of being labeled pro-black and because of a mob mentality that punishes individuals who hesitate to join a cause—no matter how violent.

Throughout section I, and later in section III, Hawkshaw represents a concept of humane justice, but he proves ineffective when pitted against McLendon, who uses the Southern culture's fears and prejudices to enrage men to commit violent acts. Hawkshaw's sense of justice is no weapon against McLendon's fierce bigotry. These two men represent diametrically opposed points of view: Hawkshaw is calm, reasonable, and just; McLendon is wild, impassioned, and sadistic. Their opposition is best expressed when Hawkshaw, responding to McLendon's goading of the men to join him in capturing Will Mayes, returns McLendon's stare without flinching. Faulkner notes of the two men, "They looked like men of different races."

When someone suggests that Miss Minnie has reported imaginary stories before, McLendon, revealing his extreme sadistic and bloodthirsty nature, replies, "What the hell difference does it make? Are you going to let the black sons get away with it until one really does it?" This statement, part of the White Goddess mentality, clearly shows that even McLendon doesn't believe the rumor. But for him and other bigots like him, a white woman's word is to be taken as the absolute and unquestionable truth. If Miss Minnie says that she was molested and the white men do nothing to punish the accused, such inaction might be interpreted to mean that the whites do not care about the well-being of Southern women. Whether or not Will Mayes attacked Miss Minnie is inconsequential so long as he is killed as an example to other black men. McLendon and his bigots are not interested in justice; they are out for blood, and nothing will satisfy them until they have murdered a black man, thus preserving the prejudices of the region.

Lest we assume that the bigoted mentality displayed by these men is limited to Jefferson, Mississippi, Faulkner includes in the barbershop scene the man whom Hawkshaw is shaving. Not from Jefferson, but from the South, the man's intolerant views demonstrate the pervasive prejudice throughout the region. Note that when the man says, "I don't live here, but by God, if our mother and wives and sisters—" he, too, subscribes to the White Goddess myth. Even more telling is his earlier comment, "Do you claim that anything excuses a nigger attacking a white woman? . . . The South dont want your kind here." He acknowledges a unique justice system based on strict racial inequality rather than on the American ideal of equal justice before the law.

By the end of section I, and before we meet Miss Minnie, many clues prove Will Mayes' innocence. Unfortunately, that Miss Minnie's reports are the result of her sexual frustrations, and that such reports have occurred before, amount to nothing in McLendon and the mob's irrational reasoning. At the very beginning, Hawkshaw says that he knows Miss Minnie, and when he maintains that nothing happened, we believe him. We rely on his opinion, especially when he points out that women like Miss Minnie tend to have fantasies and illusions about men.

Another man in the barbershop declares that the weather is so unbearable, "It's enough to make any man do anything. Even to her." This comment emphasizes Miss Minnie's failing attractiveness and society's belief—disproved by modern psychology—that physical attractiveness is a factor in rape. Although the man's comment about the weather supports the charge against Will Mayes, Miss Minnie's unattractiveness strengthens Hawkshaw's contention that she is a frustrated person who fantasizes about libidinous affairs. Likewise, we hear, "This aint the first man scare she ever had . . . " The section ends with a further note of doubt: "You reckon he really done it to her?"

Section II.   A rapid and effective transition from the tenseness of the barbershop to the outwardly peaceful life of Miss Minnie begins this section, which recounts her early social exploits and emphasizes the emptiness of her current life. Daily, she follows a purposeless and repetitive schedule of swinging on her front porch until noon, then shopping downtown in the afternoon. The "lace-trimmed boudoir cap" she wears while swinging symbolizes her pent-up sexual frustration: That she wears in public an article of clothing meant to be worn in private demonstrates her desperation to be noticed. Her life seems to be one of uselessness, perhaps due to her realization that she possesses a "faintly haggard manner" and a "bright, haggard look."

Faulkner recounts Miss Minnie's school years to stress the disparity between her youth and her present age. The importance of how she was received during her school days compared to how she is treated as a middle-aged adult cannot be overemphasized: The decline in her social popularity is a direct cause of her sexual inhibition, which is one reason for her accusing Will Mayes of raping her. When young, Miss Minnie's attractiveness "enabled her for a time to ride upon the crest of the town's social life." Growing up, her friends were unaware of her family's lower social standing in Jefferson, but they became conscious of social class as they aged and recognized that Miss Minnie was their inferior.

Although her contemporaries married, Miss Minnie did not—but not because she didn't want to. Instead, she became known as "aunty," and it wasn't until she began dating the bank cashier that she fretted about this label, asking her acquaintances to call her "cousin." Similar to the town's reaction to "poor Emily" in "A Rose for Emily," the town castigated "poor Minnie" for having an adulterous affair with the cashier, who eventually moves away.

The narration now shifts to the present time, and we see the marked change in Miss Minnie's behavior. It has been twelve years since the town relegated her to an adulteress. She now secretly sips whiskey, and her life has "a quality of furious unreality," a notable description when we remember how often McLendon is described as "furious." We know that Miss Minnie has lost her sexual appeal because when she walks downtown, the "sitting and lounging men [do] not even follow her with their eyes any more."

Much of the information supplied in this section supports the contention that Miss Minnie reports fictitious sexual encounters to reawaken the town's interest in her sexuality and to convince herself that she is attractive and desirable. Apparently, she partly accomplishes this goal; in section IV, after reporting the sexual attack, she again becomes the center of attention, and people once again look at her as a sexual woman: "Even the young men lounging in the doorway tipped their hats and followed with their eyes the motion of her hips and legs when she passed." If it were Miss Minnie's intent to regain attention for herself by reporting a sexual assault, she achieves her purpose—at the expense of Will Mayes' life.

Section III. This section returns to the actions leading up to and including the murder. Again, the weather is associated with the men's behavior. The "lifeless air," the "spent dust," and the "wan hemorrhage of the moon" emphasize the dry September, and all of these images are connected with death.

When Hawkshaw joins McLendon's group, they think that he has changed his mind and has come to join their revenge; however, Hawkshaw continues to try to convince them to stop their thirst for murder. He questions the believability of Miss Minnie's charge, pleading with the group to consider how "a lady will kind of think things about men when there aint any reason to . . . " Because his reasoning falls on deaf ears, he changes his strategy and argues that Will would have left town by now if he were guilty: He would know that he'd be punished. Hawkshaw's attempts at quelling the violence, however, are ineffectual against the men's frenzy and rage.

When the mob captures Will at his workplace, they are ready to kill him on the spot until McLendon stops them. After roughly handcuffing Will and throwing him in the car, they are so agitated that they need something on which to release their pent-up feelings. First McLendon, then the others, strike Will; in defense, Will "swept his manacled hands across their faces and slashed the barber upon the mouth." Hawkshaw strikes back instinctively, and suddenly he wants out of the car.

Hawkshaw's desire to get out of the car can be interpreted in several ways. He wants nothing to do with the violence, and he fears that in striking back at Will, he, too, is becoming emotionally caught up in the murderous fever of the others. Or, he recognizes the futility of his attempts to stop the killing and abandons all hope. Or, he fears that the men will take out part of their hatred on him, and he will be murdered with Will.

Hawkshaw jumps from the car, and the men drive on. When the car returns, Hawkshaw hides in a ditch, afraid that the mob might be hungry for more violence, this time against him. He counts only four people in the car; we know that the men have killed Will.

The relationship between the sterility of the weather and the mob's violence is masterfully detailed in this section and deserves special attention. As the men's craving for violence intensifies, so too does the weather. The "pall of dust" that characterizes the onset of night foreshadows Will's death; the day ends in a "pall," which is a cover draped over a coffin, and Will's life probably ends in the darkness of an abandoned pit. In observing that "dust hung . . . above the land," Faulkner makes Will's murder a universal event, not something confined only to Jefferson, Mississippi. The "hemorrhage" of the moon intensifies the mob's rushing to capture Will; when they force him into the car, their breathing is described as "a dry hissing," an image linked to the sound a snake makes. The men have become poisonous creatures, influenced by the malevolent weather.

Ironically, the moon's position appears to shift in direct correlation to Hawkshaw's actions. After he jumps from the moving car and is no longer part of the murderous mob, "The moon was higher, riding high and clear of the dust at last." Note, however, that the town, representative of a culture that allows the brutally violent murder of an innocent black man, "began to glare beneath the dust." Hawkshaw might be free of culpability in the killing, but the town is not.

After Will's death, the dust imagery seems almost soothing. The description of an all-encompassing dust suggests death's immortality for Will. Also, it has a settling effect after the intensely violent action we know has happened: "The dust swallowed them; the glare and the sound died away. The dust of them hung for a while, but soon the eternal dust absorbed it again." The "eternal" dust evokes our sympathy for Will and hints at an eternal afterlife for him. However, violence still lurks below the surface; nothing can forestall Miss Minnie's hysteria and McLendon's continuing rage.

Section IV. It is Saturday night, and Miss Minnie is preparing to go downtown with her friends, who are anxious to see the effects, if any, of the rape on her. Their baiting her with questions demonstrates that they are more interested in juicy, sensational gossip than with genuine concern and affection for her: "When you have had time to get over the shock, you must tell us what happened. What he said and did, everything." She has aroused the interest of the curiosity seekers, but this section reemphasizes her many frustrations despite having regained all kinds of attention.

As Miss Minnie and her friends walk downtown, young people observe her with sexual curiosity. The image of her friends talking in voices that sound like "long, hovering sighs of hissing exultation" recalls the snake-like lust of Will's killers and suggests that these "friends" are little better than McLendon and his gang.

Knowledge of Will's disappearance has become widespread, for Miss Minnie's friends note, "There's not a Negro on the square. Not one." Here, Faulkner is commenting on a unique Southern phenomenon: Saturday is traditionally the day that many Southern blacks spend in town. But when something violent occurs, such as a rape or a murder, the entire black community reacts by disappearing, or, in Southern idiom, by becoming invisible.

The scene in the theater pits Miss Minnie against the unreality of the movie's fantasy world, where life "began to unfold, beautiful and passionate and sad." Her false sexuality is juxtaposed against the many pairs of young lovers, who enter the theater "scented and sibilant," an image that again emphasizes the snake-like quality of Jefferson's citizens. The movie represents an escape from life's burdens, but, instead, Miss Minnie begins to laugh hysterically, implying that either she recognizes finally the futility of reclaiming a sexual identity or she might very well be suffering a nervous collapse, or both.

The section ends with the friends undressing Miss Minnie and perversely examining her hair for signs of gray. Faulkner's description of the friends' eyes as "darkly aglitter, secret and passionate," suggests that Miss Minnie is not the only Southern woman who is sexually repressed. Still wondering if the rape truly occurred, the women are not convinced of Miss Minnie's accusations, but Will Mayes has had to pay for these charges with his life.

Section V. "Dry September" closes with John McLendon's returning to his "birdcage" home at midnight and brutally confronting his wife. Hearing his question, "Haven't I told you about sitting up like this, waiting to see when I come in?" we wonder where and what he must have been doing the other times, and how often his wife must endure his abusive behavior. The sadism that was revealed in his slashing out at Will continues in his sadistic treatment of his wife when he "half struck, half flung her across the chair."

Mrs. McLendon's seemingly passive acceptance of her husband's abuse increases our sympathy for her. By ending the story with such a disturbing view of her as a victim, Faulkner reiterates the victimization of many of his characters, most especially Will. Our final glimpse of McLendon is not of the heroic American decorated for valor, but of a mean, vicious, and violently sadistic bigot. Ironically, he kills a man to protect the so-called sanctity of Southern white women, yet he treats his own wife as a piece of property, to do with as he pleases. The White Goddess concept is an abstract ideal, and that is all it is—an ideal that fails miserably in real life.

- **vitiated**   of poor quality; debased.

- **pomade**   a perfumed ointment used to groom hair.

- **drummer**   a salesman who peddles his wares in various towns.

- **voile dresses** dresses made out of lightweight fabric, such as cotton or silk.

- **porticoes** roofed porches.

- **a red runabout** a red convertible.

- **serried** tightly pressed rows.

- **the sons** When this short story was published, the era prohibited magazines from printing "the sons of bitches."

- **nimbused** refers to the cloudy circle of light around a lamp, especially in fog.

"SPOTTED HORSES"

"Spotted Horses" is one of Faulkner's finest examples of his unique type of local color. Critics familiar with American Old Southwest humor will recognize his indebtedness to this brand of tall-tale humor, which relies almost entirely on a liberally exaggerated oral narration. In the short story, Faulkner utilizes a sewing machine agent as the oral narrator to create an informal, chatty, conversational tone.

In addition to this narrative style, Faulkner uses other classical types and techniques of humor in his storytelling; here, he uses a traditional character known as the con man, someone who captures a person's confidence—from which we get the word "con"—in order to take advantage of that person's gullibility. There are many variations of the con man, but in all cases the con man's success depends on the greed of his victim; a good con man will know intuitively which approach of deception will be the most successful. For example, in "Spotted Horses," the Texan knows that Henry Armstid is not going to allow Eck Snopes to buy a horse for a mere two dollars, especially since the Texan has already given Eck a free horse.

In this particular short story, we have three types of con men: the sewing machine agent, the Texan, and Flem Snopes, and each of these con men displays his con artistry differently. The sewing machine agent is unassuming; the Texan redeems himself; and Flem is a schemer who lies adeptly.

The central narrator, a mild-mannered con man with something of a conscience, is a perfect narrator because, as an itinerant sewing machine agent, he himself knows the value of a con game. Because

Flem Snopes once took advantage of him, he has a grudging admiration for anyone who is sharp enough to get the best of him. As a con artist himself, he recognizes and admires Flem's superiority, although he despises Flem's inhumanity.

The Texan is a traditional con man. He plays the game of selling horses and enjoys his triumphs, but he is not as vicious as Flem. When he sees how disturbingly calm and defeated Mrs. Armstid is about her husband's squandering their last five dollars, he attempts to restore the money. He responds to her human needs and tries to lessen the hardships and pain caused by her rashly impractical, abusive husband.

Comparing Mrs. Armstid's treatment by the Texan and how she is treated by Flem, the narrator reveals that Flem is a third type of con man, one who is mean, vicious, and unerringly inhumane. He does not soil his hands by directly involving himself in any dirty work. Instead, he sits apart from the entire transaction. His omnipotence and omnipresence, felt constantly throughout the story, are emphasized by the narrator's often-reiterated phrases, "That Flem" and "Them Snopes."

A key ingredient in Old Southwest humor is incongruity, or the juxtaposition of contrasting elements. For example, the narrator describes the Texas ponies in these terms: "They was colored like parrots and they was quiet as doves, and ere a one of them would kill you quick as a rattlesnake." The first two statements conjure a lovely, quiet image of beauty and peacefulness, but this idyllic image contrasts with the third statement—that the horses would kill a person as quickly as a rattlesnake would. To describe the animals as "ponies" is, in itself, absurdly incongruous because the word "pony" evokes a benign, sweet, lovable, and tame animal, which is the opposite of these wild, vicious, and untamable beasts.

Another quality of Old Southwest humor is exaggeration, which Faulkner certainly uses when he describes the horses' wild "cattymount" behavior. For example, our first glimpse of the animals involves the sewing machine agent's unexpected run-in with them at the beginning of the story: "Here I was this morning pretty near half way to town, with the team ambling along and me, setting in the buckboard about half asleep when all of a sudden something come surging up outen the bushes and jumped the road clean, without touching hoof to it. It flew right over my team big as a billboard and flying through the air like a hawk." Such observations create an unbelievability, which is characteristic of the tall tale. Certainly the agent's taking "thirty minutes to stop my team" after the horses jump over him enhances the tale's comic quality.

"Spotted Horses" was first published in *Scribner's Magazine* for June 1931. Faulkner included an expanded version of the story in his novel *The Hamlet* (1940). This expanded version includes as its last section a courtroom scene in which Mrs. Armstid sues Flem Snopes for five dollars, and Mrs. Tull sues Eck Snopes for damages sustained by her husband. Both suits are dismissed after neither woman can prove who owns the horses. The discussion in these Notes follows the text originally published in *Scribner's*, which is anthologized more often than the longer text.

Part I. Behind the extravagance of the narrative situations, the humorous narration itself, and the comic techniques, there is a more serious intent to "Spotted Horses." With all of the different character types found in the story—from the rational narrator, to the mild, meek, and down-trodden Mrs. Armstid, to the strong and determined Mrs. Littlejohn, to Ad, the half-wit son of Eck Snopes, and to the amoral Flem Snopes—we have a magnificent cross section of rural persons who inhabit Yoknapatawpha County. There are also strong implications that things are out of control in this particular community.

The narrator, V. K. Ratliff, is not named in this particular story, but Faulkner uses this itinerant sewing machine agent as a character in most of his stories involving the Snopes. The opinions Ratliff expresses are those felt by most readers—for example, his view of Flem Snopes: "That Flem Snopes. I be dog if he ain't a case, now." The story's unity lies partly in the fact that this same incredulity concerning Flem is expressed at the end of the story, first by I. O. Snopes—"You can't git ahead of Flem. You can't touch him. Ain't he a sight, now?"—and then by Ratliff, who maintains that if he were to do what Flem does, he would be lynched.

Among the things that surprise Ratliff is the cool manner in which Flem enters the community and immediately begins greedily accumulating money, first as a clerk in the Varner store, and then by marrying Varner's daughter, Eula. Once Flem has a foothold in the county, Ratliff believes that in ten years he will own everything.

After narrating the history of Flem's establishing himself in the county, Ratliff tells us about Eula Varner, describing her as "one of these here kind of big, soft-looking gals that could giggle richer than plowed new-ground." "Young bucks" swarm around her like "bees around a honey pot," but it is Flem who marries her. The couple disappears after their marriage, and when Eula returns—without Flem—she has a child with her. Ratliff reports on the amazing abilities of this child: According to the marriage date, he is supposed to be three months old, but he can already pull himself upright, hanging onto a chair. Ratliff thinks that at that speed, the child could be "chewing tobacco and voting time it's eight years old." Obviously, Eula was already several months pregnant at the time of her wedding.

Soon afterward, Flem returns to the county with a Texan and about "two dozen of them Texas ponies, hitched to one another with barbed wire." This unusual tethering device showcases these animals as anything but typical "ponies." That evening, as people sit on Mrs. Littlejohn's boardinghouse porch and listen to the "spotted varmints swirling," the serenity of the community is interrupted forever.

Although Flem denies ownership of the ponies, it is clear to everyone that he is involved in the shady transaction of selling them. His ultimate desire is to control the village, and one way he goes about this is by introducing disorder—here, represented by the horses—into the peaceful community.

Faulkner's treatment of the Snopes family in this first section is most effective when we note the animal imagery associated with the Snopeses. Part of this imagery involves juxtaposing the horses' physical abnormalities with those of the Snopeses. For example, not only does the parrot-like, spotted coloring of the horses suggest that something is wrong with them, but Ratliff draws special attention to their mismatched eyes. He comments, "Nere a one of them had two eyes the same color . . . " These physical irregularities are matched by Eula's child, although the child's physical abilities are normal for a toddler older than three months. However, by exaggerating the child's physical abilities, Ratliff comically suggests that something is wrong with him.

The wild nature of the Snopes clan, most of whom are transient sharecroppers who "never stayed on any place over a year," is intensified by the extreme agitation of the horses. Readers should note how the Snopeses' birthing process is characterized: " . . . the twins of that year's litter" and "It was a regular nest of them." Every single thing and person is out of control in this section, including the Snopeses and horses alike.

Part II. This section opens by reemphasizing that no one knows if Flem owns the spotted horses or not. Ratliff points out that even Flem's cousin, Eck, does not know, which does not surprise Ratliff given that "Flem would skin Eck quick as he would ere a one of us."

By sun-up on the day of the auction, there is a crowd waiting for the sale to begin, and Flem is nowhere to be found. Although Ratliff doesn't draw special attention to this fact, twice in this section he notes that the auction's attendees have brought their "seed-money" with them, money intended to buy seeds for planting the crops that will support them for the next year. In this otherwise serene community, the auction appears to make people lose their sensibilities and gamble with their futures.

At first, no one will bid on a horse—perhaps because the horses act unnaturally wild and look untamable. The Texan, who is running the auction, appeals to Eck, but Eck is afraid to bid. To prove that the ponies are tame, the Texan jumps in among them, and he is lost—forever, it seems—among dust, clouds, and total confusion. When he finally gains control over one of the animals, the image of him amongst the horses involves animal imagery similar to the earlier images of the Snopeses: "His neck swole up like a spreading adder's . . . "

While everyone's attention is focused on the Texan, Henry and his wife, Mrs. Armstid, arrive. The Texan shows his skill as a con man when Henry orders his wife to "Git on back to that wagon." She pathetically pleads with her husband not to bid on a horse, and immediately the Texan recognizes the probably long-standing conflict of wills between the husband and wife, which he will take advantage of in order to coax Henry into buying a horse. The Texan's actions demonstrate that he is an excellent con man because he can so readily and easily pick out his victims. However, we hear Ratliff—and then Mrs. Armstid—emphasize that the family is in desperate financial straits, and, as we learn later, the Texan begins to sympathize with Mrs. Armstid's plight. She also evokes our pity when she whines that Henry "haint no more despair than to buy one of them things," and Ratliff confirms that she supports the family by weaving by firelight after everyone is asleep. Ironically, Mrs. Armstid's pleading with her husband reveals that the couple has five dollars, information that the Texan will remember when the bidding begins.

The Texan, summing up the situation, offers Eck one free horse if he will start the bidding on the next one. Understanding his audience's basic greed, he knows that a greedy person resents someone else's getting something for free. He is a sharp manipulator in the tradition of the successful con man. When the Texan accepts Eck's bid of two dollars for the next horse, he plays his audience quite easily by asking, "Are you boys going to stand there and see Eck get two horses at a dollar a head?" Summing up the situation, Ratliff points out, "That done it. I be dog if he wasn't nigh as smart as Flem Snopes." Ratliff admires the shrewd operator and the superb con man.

The bidding begins: Henry bids three dollars, and Eck, forgetting that he doesn't want one of the creatures, bids four; Henry offers a final bid of five dollars, the sum total of his wife's savings. The strong, brutal Henry prevails over his meek, subservient wife, who again pleads with the Texan not to take the bid and then threatens, "It'll be a curse onto you and yourn during all the time of man."

Part III. It takes all day to sell the horses, most of which go for three or four dollars, less than the five dollars that Henry paid for his. After the auction, Henry is impatient to get his horse, and when the Texan refuses to help him catch it, Henry orders Mrs. Armstid, who has been sitting in their wagon, to bring the plowline rope. Ratliff describes Mrs. Armstid as "not looking at nothing, ever since this morning." She is a defeated woman; all financial security for her family seems lost because of her husband's arrogant stupidity.

The Texan tries to prevent Mrs. Armstid from going inside the corral, but she obeys her husband. Twice Henry blames her for letting the horse escape, and twice he hits her with the rope. Before he can hit her a third time, the Texan interferes, stopping Henry's sadistic beating. He leads Henry out of the lot and gives back the five dollars to Mrs. Armstid. Infuriated, Henry demands his horse. He grabs the five dollars from Mrs. Armstid and gives it to Flem, who has finally turned up at the auction. The Texan tells Mrs. Armstid that she can get her money from Flem. This action sets up the final encounter between Mrs. Armstid and Flem, an encounter we know will be doomed to failure for Mrs. Armstid.

Part IV. This is the most hilarious section of the story, mainly because the humor is based on exaggeration and our responses to these outrageous situations. Faulkner uses exaggeration extensively to describe the impossible agility and magic-like feats of the wild horses, and he incorporates many similes in order to create the soaring, comical moments. For example, at first Mrs. Littlejohn is frightened for Eck Snopes' boy, Ad, who gets dangerously close to the wild horses. But she is told that Ad lives a "charmed life"—the life of the innocent—because the horses the night before "jumped clean over that boy's head and never touched him." Likewise, the downtrodden Mrs. Armstid also lives a charmed life: When Henry tries to catch his horse, the horses bolt and trample over him, breaking his leg; "like a creek flood," they tear up everything in their path, except Mrs. Armstid, who sits in her wagon like something "carved outen wood."

One of the most hilarious scenes records Eck's horse galloping up the front stairs of Mrs. Littlejohn's porch and into her house. Charging against the melodeon, which makes a sound "like a railroad engine," it then encounters Ratliff in his longjohn underwear. Ratliff swears that the horse looks like "a fourteen-foot pinwheel a-blaring its eyes at me." Convinced that this wild animal has never before seen a sewing machine agent in underclothes, he jumps out of a window. The horse clatters up the hall and runs into Mrs. Littlejohn, who has clean washing in one hand and her washboard in the other. She swats the horse on the head, and as it turns around, she swats it on the rump. The horse leaves, again missing Ad by soaring over the boy's head "without touching a hair." Apparently, the horse is discriminating enough not to hurt young children—Ad—or downtrodden women—Mrs. Armstid.

Ratliff's exaggerated description of the horse's unlikely course of flight adds to the already hilarious scene. The horse jumps over the porch's banisters and fences "like a hen-hawk" and flies over "eight or ten upside-down wagons." Going about "forty miles a hour," it comes to the bridge on which Vernon Tull and his family sit in their wagon. The wild horse climbs up the wagon tongue "like a squirrel," and the tame mules pulling the wagon turn themselves around and follow the horse, overturning the wagon.

Part V. This section recounts the immediate aftermath of the horses' escaping into the countryside. Henry Armstid is discovered amidst the trash in the feed lot with his leg broken. He is carried to

Mrs. Littlejohn's, who sends for Will Varner, a veterinarian who also practices medicine on people. Mrs. Littlejohn maintains that "a man ain't so different from a mule, come long come short. Except maybe a mule's got more sense." Her comments are apt given the men's gullibility at the auction and her own actions during the sale. Throughout the story, she has seemed to be a no-nonsense woman, who sets about her chores and doesn't get suckered into Flem and the Texan's scheme. As the next section shows, she is a foil for Mrs. Armstid.

Constantly in the background, the horses are heard running across fields and bridges. Henry feels the pain from his broken leg—and from Will Varner's not using any "chloryfoam" to set the leg—and begins screaming. Along with Mrs. Littlejohn, we do not feel much pity for Henry's suffering because he more or less deserves what he gets.

During the entire episode, nothing is heard from Flem Snopes. In fact, he hasn't been seen since the auction.

Part VI. The opening of this section reveals Mrs. Armstid's inability to act. The contrast between her and Mrs. Littlejohn is significant in that Mrs. Littlejohn has always been in complete control of her life and acts firmly and determinedly. Mrs. Armstid is inconsistent and indecisive, but we cannot severely fault her for this—given the abusive relationship she is in.

The meeting between the two women is comic only in how Ratliff reports it. Mrs. Littlejohn tells Mrs. Armstid that Flem Snopes is back in town, and that she can now ask him for the five dollars, to which Mrs. Armstid asks apprehensively, "You reckon he'll give it to me?" Although Mrs. Littlejohn does not believe that Flem will refund the money, she hopes that Mrs. Armstid's asking for it might shame him.

Throughout this conversation, Ratliff notes that Mrs. Littlejohn washes dishes "like a man, like they was made out of iron." The women's conversation is sprinkled with Ratliff's observations about the dish washing. As Mrs. Armstid whines about whether or not Flem will return her money, Ratliff records Mrs. Littlejohn's impatience by noting how she treats the dishes: "It sounded like she was throwing the dishes at one another," and "Then it sounded like Mrs. Littlejohn taken up all the dishes and throwed them at the cookstove." Finally, Mrs. Littlejohn loses all patience. She tells Mrs. Armstid that she would give the money to Henry to buy another horse—if only she could be sure that this time the horse would kill him.

The scene shifts to the front door of the country store, where Flem sits whittling. The image of him carving wood recalls that Mrs. Armstid has constantly been referred to as being made "outen wood." In this final scene, we will see her being whittled away metaphorically by Flem.

For Flem's last triumph, he is surrounded by other Snopeses, including Eck Snopes, I. O. Snopes, and Ad Snopes. Many of I. O. Snopes' actions resemble animal behavior: "He had been rubbing his back up and down on the door, but he stopped now, watching Flem like a pointing dog"; and "I. O. cackled, like a hen, slapping his legs with both hands." When Ratliff sees Mrs. Armstid coming up the road, he begins to taunt Flem about the transaction with Mrs. Armstid. His comment, "Well, if a man can't take care of himself in a trade, he can't blame the man that trims him," emphasizes one important aspect of literature that deals with con artists: People who allow themselves to be tricked or gypped deserve what they get.

Ratliff, who is sympathetic to Mrs. Armstid's downtrodden state, points out that Henry never bought a horse, and that the Texan told Mrs. Armstid to get her money back from Flem. When the men become aware of the approaching Mrs. Armstid, I. O. Snopes suggests that Flem leave by the back door, but he does not. When she addresses him about the money, "Flem looked up. The knife never stopped. It went on trimming . . . " He tells her that the Texan took the money with him, and that there is nothing he can do. Another pitiful entreaty by Mrs. Armstid elicits the same response.

As Mrs. Armstid turns to leave, Flem tells her to wait a minute. He goes inside the store, and we assume that Flem has had a change of heart and will return the five dollars. However, he returns with a small sack of candy, which he did not pay for, and gives it to her, saying, "A little sweetening for the chaps." Our surprise at his audacious, incorrigible behavior is beyond description.

Ratliff reports that as Mrs. Armstid leaves, she "looked like a old snag still standing up and moving along on a high water." She might be "still standing," but obviously she is a defeated woman. Four times in this section Ratliff characterizes her as "not looking at nothing." Her faded sunbonnet presents an image of a woman whose spirit is worn away.

Meantime, Flem opens his knife, resumes his whittling, and spits after her. The wood imagery, his whittling, and finally his spitting emphasize Flem's despicable and uncaring nature. The Snopes kin, especially I. O. Snopes, are proud of Flem's ability to con people, and V. K. Ratliff is simply puzzled.

- **buckboard** an open buggy.

- **skun** skinned; here, meaning "bested" because of clever trading.

- **curried** A currycomb is a comb with metal teeth used to groom horses; a horse that has been combed is considered "curried."

- **shell corn** feed corn that has been removed from the cob.

- **cattymounts** wild felines: mountain lions; short for "catamountains." Here, the spotted horses are called "cattymounts" because of their wild behavior.

- **adder** a type of snake, usually with a zigzag black band running along its back; the Texan's neck swelling like a "spreading adder" refers to the puff adder, a large and dangerous snake that "puffs" its body below the head when threatened.

- **holp** helped.

- **frailed** whipped.

- **water moccasin** a poisonous snake found in southern states, often around creeks and swamps.

- **melodeon** a small, musical organ.

- **pinwheel** a toy consisting of colored paper or plastic pinned to a stick so that it revolves when blown.

- **toted** carried.

- **grip** a small piece of luggage about the size of a gym bag.

- **snag** a broken tree limb.

CRITICAL ESSAY

FAULKNER'S STYLE

Faulkner's style in his short stories is not the typical Faulknerian stream-of-conscious narration found in his major novels. However, some of his novels' narrative techniques are also present in the stories and include extended descriptions and details, actions in one scene that then recall a past or future scene, and complex sentence structure. What is important to remember is that Faulkner always has a purpose in choosing which different stylistic technique to use at which point in his stories: The narrative devices mirror the psychological complexity of the short stories' characters and settings.

One of the most effective ways Faulkner establishes depth of character and scene is by using long lists of descriptions. Oftentimes, a description of an object will be followed by a description of a character: In this way, the object and character, because they have been similarly described, take on the appearance of each other. For example, at the beginning of "A Rose for Emily," Faulkner describes the Grierson house: "It was a big, squarish frame house that had once been white, decorated with cupolas and spires and scrolled balconies in the heavily lightsome style of the seventies, set on what had once been our most select street." Following this, Faulkner then characterizes Miss Emily, and the "heavily lightsome" style of the house parallels her physical appearance: Her skeleton is "small and spare"—"lightsome"—yet, because of her slight figure, "what would have been merely plumpness in another was obesity in her"— "heavily lightsome." The woman and the house she lived in her entire life are inseparable. Both are now dead—she literally, the house figuratively—but even in their deaths they are described as physically similar: The house is "filled with dust and shadows," and she dies with "her gray head propped on a pillow yellow and moldy with age and lack of sunlight." Stylistically, the "yellow and moldy with age and lack of sunlight" describes the house, the pillow, and Miss Emily, all ancient relics of a time long past.

Another example of Faulkner's using extended descriptions is in "That Evening Sun," in which the first two paragraphs describe the town of Jefferson in the present and in the past. The first paragraph, one long sentence, portrays the town's present condition: The streets are paved, there is electricity, and black women still wash white people's laundry, but now they transport themselves and the laundry in automobiles. The second paragraph, like the first, is one complete sentence, but it portrays Jefferson's past: The shade trees, which in the present have been cut down to make room for electrical poles, still stand, and the black women who wash for white people carry the laundry in bundles on their heads, not in automobiles. By juxtaposing these two paragraphs, with their lengthy descriptions of Jefferson, Faulkner establishes one of the major themes found throughout all of his short stories, the difference between the present and the past, and how that difference affects people in dissimilar ways. We are reminded of section V in "A Rose for Emily," in which that section's second paragraph, composed of a short sentence and then a very lengthy one, describes how old-timers, "confusing time with its mathematical progression," psychologically still live in the past even though a "narrow bottle-neck of the most recent decade of years" separates them from it.

Because many of the short stories juxtapose past conditions with the present and include jumping between different times, Faulkner needed a narrative technique that would seamlessly tie one scene to another. His solution was to make an object or action in one scene trigger another scene in which that same object or action was present. For example, in "A Rose for Emily," the new aldermen's attempting to collect Miss Emily's taxes prompts the narrator to recall another scene thirty years earlier, when Miss Emily's neighbors complain that a smell is coming from her property, and they want the city fathers to do something about it. Faulkner links these two scenes by simply using the same verb—"vanquished"—to describe Miss Emily's actions: "So she vanquished them, horse and foot, just as she had vanquished their fathers thirty years before about the smell."

Stylistically, Faulkner is best known for his complex sentence structure. Generally, the more complex the sentence structure, the more psychologically complex a character's thoughts. Such is the case in "Barn Burning," in which young Sarty Snopes is torn between being loyal to his father and doing what he innately senses is right. This conflict culminates in Sarty's warning Major de Spain that his father is going to burn the major's barn.

It is after Sarty warns de Spain and then runs toward the major's barn that we have one of the best examples of Faulkner's narrative complexity. The third paragraph from the story's end hinges on Sarty's running, just as the paragraph's last sentence itself seems to run on and on. The preceding sentence reads, "So he ran down the drive, blood and breath roaring; presently he was in the road again though he could not see." Coupled with this blindness is Sarty's loss of hearing: He is so caught up in his conflicting loyalties—and, perhaps, the guilt he might feel for being disloyal to his father—that he temporarily loses his physical senses.

Additionally, Faulkner emphasizes Sarty's psychological instability in this energized scene with descriptive terms that suggest Sarty's increasing confusion. Even before Sarty hears gun shots, he is "wild" with grief as the "furious silhouette" of de Spain's horse thunders by. When he hears the shots, he instinctively cries out to his father and then begins to run. Faulkner intensifies the scene by repeating the verb "run" and quickens the pace by including words that end in "ing": " . . . running again before he knew he had begun to run, stumbling, tripping over something and scrabbling up again without ceasing to run, looking backward over his shoulder at the glare as he got up, running on among the invisible trees, panting, sobbing, 'Father! Father!'" The sentence builds and builds, faster and faster, until it culminates in Sarty's desperate cry to his father, who he fears has been killed. The increasing intensity of the sentence mirrors the young boy's increasing concern for his father's safety.

Another example of Faulkner's complex sentence structure is in "Dry September," in which a lynch mob led by John McLendon kills Will Mayes, a black man who they suspect raped Miss Minnie, a white woman. In part, the weather is to blame for the mob's irrational behavior; it has not rained in sixty-two days. Faulkner creates sentences that, through a series of interrupting phrases, emphasize the weather's effect on the townspeople. One example of this technique is the last sentence in the story's opening paragraph. Rearranged so that the subject phrase and verb stand side by side, the sentence reads, "Attacked, insulted, frightened: none of them knew exactly what had happened." However, Faulkner hints that the dry weather has clouded the men's logical thinking by interjecting between the subject phrase and the verb numerous descriptions about the stagnant air and the stagnant minds of the men. These phrases include " . . . the ceiling fan stirred, without freshening it, the vitiated air, sending back upon them, in recurrent surges of stale pomade and lotion, their own stale breath and odor . . . " Stylistically, these descriptions interrupt the sentence's natural progression of subject-verb and emphasize the weather's negative effect on the men gathered in the barbershop.

Part of Faulkner's greatness lies in his style and the way he adjusts this style to fit the subject under narration. He can adapt a more traditional type of writing to his stories—as he does in "Spotted Horses," in which he uses the Old Southwest humor formula of writing—as easily as he can invent new, complicated narrative techniques. Whichever he chooses, his style parallels the complexity of his characters and gives a unique flavor to his short stories.

REVIEW QUESTIONS AND ESSAY TOPICS

(1). Discuss the narrative structure of "A Rose for Emily." Why does Faulkner present the story's events in non-chronological order? Would the story be successful if he had told it in a strictly linear fashion? Why or why not?

(2). How does the narrator's opinion of Miss Emily change throughout "A Rose for Emily"? Does the narrator's admiring her, even after she kills Homer Barron and sleeps with his corpse, bother you? What does the narrator's accepting Miss Emily's actions suggest about Southern culture?

(3). Compare how the townspeople treat Miss Emily in "A Rose for Emily" and Miss Minnie in "Dry September."

(4). How does Mrs. Compson's whining throughout "That Evening Sun" fit into the White Goddess concept discussed in the commentary about the story?

(5). Discuss Nancy's threatening Jesus in "That Evening Sun" if she found him cheating on her with another woman. Is it fair that Jesus threatens Nancy for doing the same? Would his killing Nancy be too extreme a punishment for her actions?

(6). Does Jesus kill Nancy at the end of "That Evening Sun"? Support why you believe he does or does not.

(7). Does Quentin mature during "That Evening Sun"? Support your answer by giving examples from the story.

(8). Discuss Sarty's mother and aunt in "Barn Burning." What are their roles in the story?

(9). Sarty is alone at the end of "Barn Burning." What do you think he will do now? What would you do?

(10). Discuss Sarty's maturing in "Barn Burning." How does it differ from Quentin's in "That Evening Sun"?

(11). Sarty's father, Abner, is very class conscious. Compare how class affects his, Major de Spain's, and Mr. Harris' actions.

(12). In "Dry September," many characters comment on the weather. How does Faulkner characterize the weather? Does it affect people's actions in the story? Has it ever affected yours?

(13). Compare Hawkshaw and McLendon in "Dry September." Is Hawkshaw's striking Will Mayes in the car comparable to McLendon's violent actions? Why does Hawkshaw strike Will?

(14). Did Miss Minnie lie in "Dry September" about Will Mayes raping her? Support your answer with examples from the story.

(15). Research the occurrence of lynchings and murders of blacks during Reconstruction. Has Faulkner overly fictionalized the murder of Will Mayes and the events surrounding it in "Dry September"?

(16). How is "Spotted Horses" an example of American Old Southwest humor?

(17). Compare V. K. Ratliff, the Texan, and Flem Snopes in "Spotted Horses." Which of these three con men is least offensive? Most offensive? Why?

(18). Discuss Henry and Mrs. Armstid's relationship in "Spotted Horses." Is Henry's treatment of his wife more cruel than McLendon's treatment of his wife in "Dry September"? Why or why not?

(19). How does Faulkner use animal imagery in "Spotted Horses"? Is it effective? Is it linked especially with any group of people?

(20). Compare Mrs. Armstid and Mrs. Littlejohn in "Spotted Horses." Does the comparison increase or decrease your opinion of Mrs. Armstid?

(21). Discuss the mob mentality in two of Faulkner's short stories. What are the characteristics he associates with this mentality?

(22). In his Nobel Prize for literature acceptance speech, Faulkner says that humanity will endure. Do his short stories suggest this optimism? Which of the stories' characters most successfully endure their hardships? Which the least?

FAULKNER'S PUBLISHED WORKS

NOVELS

Soldiers' Pay (1926)
Mosquitoes (1927)
Sartoris (1929)
The Sound and the Fury (1929)
As I Lay Dying (1930)
Sanctuary (1931)
Idyll in the Desert (1931)
Light in August (1932)
Pylon (1935)
Absalom, Absalom! (1936)
The Unvanquished (1938)
The Wild Palms (1939)
The Hamlet (1940)
Go Down, Moses (1942)
Intruder in the Dust (1945)
A Fable (1954)
The Town (1957)
The Mansion (1959)
The Reivers (1962)
Flags in the Dust (1973)

POETRY

The Marble Faun (1924)
Salmagundi (1932)
This Earth (1932)
A Green Bough (1933)

SHORT STORY COLLECTIONS

These Thirteen (1931)
Miss Zilphia Gant (1932)
Doctor Martino and Other Stories (1934)
Knight's Gambit (1949)
Collected Stories of William Faulkner (1950)
Big Woods (1955)
Selected Short Stories of William Faulkner (1961)
Uncollected Short Stories of William Faulkner (1979)

DRAMA

Requiem for a Nun (1951)

PRODUCED SCREENPLAYS

Today We Live (1933)
The Road to Glory (1936)
To Have and Have Not (1945)
The Big Sleep (1946)
Land of the Pharaohs (1955)

SELECTED BIBLIOGRAPHY

GENERAL

BLOTNER, JOSEPH. *Faulkner. A Biography*. New York: Random House, 1984.

CAROTHERS, JAMES B. *William Faulkner's Short Stories*. Ann Arbor, Michigan: UMI Research Press, 1985.

FOWLER, DOREEN, and ANN J. ABADIE, eds. *Faulkner and Humor*. Jackson: University Press of Mississippi, 1986.

_____. *Faulkner and the Craft of Fiction*. Jackson: University Press of Mississippi, 1987.

GWYNN, FREDERICK L., and JOSEPH L. BLOTNER, eds. *Faulkner in the University. Class Conferences at the University of Virginia 1957–1958*. Charlottesville: University of Virginia Press, 1959.

HARRINGTON, EVANS, and ANN J. ABADIE, eds. *Faulkner and the Short Story*. Jackson: University Press of Mississippi, 1992.

_____. *The Maker and the Myth: Faulkner and Yoknapatawpha*. Jackson: University Press of Mississippi, 1978.

KARL, FREDERICK R. *William Faulkner: American Writer. A Biography*. New York: Weidenfeld & Nicolson, 1989.

KINNEY, ARTHUR F., ed. *Critical Essays on William Faulkner: The Compson Family*. Boston: G. K. Hall, 1982.

_____. *Critical Essays on William Faulkner: The Sartoris Family*. Boston: G. K. Hall, 1985.

MINTER, DAVID L. *William Faulkner: The Writing of a Life*. Baltimore: Johns Hopkins University Press, 1980.

WASSON, BEN. *Count No 'Count: Flashbacks to Faulkner*. Jackson: University Press of Mississippi, 1983.

"A ROSE FOR EMILY"

ALLEN, DENNIS W. "Horror and Perverse Delight: Faulkner's 'A Rose for Emily.'" *Modern Fiction Studies* 30.4 (1984): 685–96.

BURDUCK, MICHAEL L. "Another View of Faulkner's Narrator in 'A Rose for Emily.'" *University of Mississippi Studies in English* 8 (1990): 209–11.

HAYS, PETER L. "Who is Faulkner's Emily?" *Studies in American Fiction* 16.1 (1988): 105–10.

JACOBS, JOHN T. "Ironic Allusions in 'A Rose for Emily.'" *Notes on Mississippi Writers* 14.2 (1982): 77–79.

LITTLER, FRANK A. "The Tangled Thread of Time: Faulkner's 'A Rose for Emily.'" *Notes on Mississippi Writers* 14.2 (1982): 80–86.

MOORE, GENE M. "Of Time and Its Mathematical Progression: Problems of Chronology in Faulkner's 'A Rose for Emily.'" *Studies in Short Fiction* 29.2 (1992): 195–204.

RODGERS, LAWRENCE R. "We All Said, 'She Will Kill Herself': The Narrator/Detective in William Faulkner's 'A Rose for Emily.'" *Clues: A Journal of Detection* 16.1 (1995): 117–29.

SCHWAB, MILINDA. "A Watch for Emily." *Studies in Short Fiction* 28.2 (1991): 215–17.

"THAT EVENING SUN"

BENNETT, KEN. "The Language of the Blues in Faulkner's 'That Evening Sun.'" *Mississippi Quarterly* 38.3 (1985): 339–42.

KUYK, DIRK, JR., et al. "Black Culture in William Faulkner's 'That Evening Sun.'" *Journal of American Studies* 20.1 (1986): 33–50.

PERRINE, LAURENCE. "'That Evening Sun': A Skein of Uncertainties." *Studies in Short Fiction* 22.3 (1985): 295–307.

PITCHER, E. W. "Motive and Metaphor in Faulkner's 'That Evening Sun.'" *Studies in Short Fiction* 18.2 (1981): 131–35.

SLABEY, ROBERT M. "Faulkner's Nancy as 'Tragic Mulatto.'" *Studies in Short Fiction* 27.3 (1990): 409–13.

"BARN BURNING"

BILLINGLEA, OLIVER. "Fathers and Sons: The Spiritual Quest in Faulkner's 'Barn Burning.'" *Mississippi Quarterly* 44.3 (1991): 287–308.

BRADFORD, M. E. "Family and Community in Faulkner's 'Barn Burning.'" *The Southern Review* 17.2 (1981): 332–39.

CACKETT, KATHY. "'Barn Burning': Debating the American Adam." *Notes on Mississippi Writers* (1989): 1–17.

FOWLER, VIRGINIA C. "Faulkner's 'Barn Burning': Sarty's Conflict Reconsidered." *College Language Association Journal* 24.4 (1981): 513–22.

HALL, JOAN WYLIE. "Faulkner's Barn Burners: Ab Snopes and the Duke of Marlborough." *Notes on Mississippi Writers* 21.2 (1989): 65–68.

HILES, JANE. "Kinship and Heredity in Faulkner's 'Barn Burning.'" *Mississippi Quarterly* 38.3 (1985): 329–37.

YUNIS, SUSAN S. "The Narrator of Faulkner's 'Barn Burning.'" *The Faulkner Journal* 6.2 (1991): 23–31.

ZENDER, KARL F. "Character and Symbol in 'Barn Burning.'" *College Literature* 16.1 (1989): 48–59.

"DRY SEPTEMBER"

CRANE, JOHN K. "But the Days Grow Short: A Reinterpretation of Faulkner's 'Dry September.'" *Twentieth Century Literature* 31.4 (1985): 410–20.

DESSNER, LAWRENCE JAY. "William Faulkner's 'Dry September': Decadence Domesticated." *College Literature* 11.2 (1984): 151–62.

VOLPE, EDMOND L. "'Dry September': Metaphor for Despair." *College Literature* 16.1 (1989): 60–65.

"SPOTTED HORSES"

EDDINS, DWIGHT. "Metahumor in Faulkner's 'Spotted Horses.'" *ARIEL* 13.1 (1982): 23–31.

RAMSEY, ALLEN. "'Spotted Horses' and Spotted Pups." *The Faulkner Journal* 5.2 (1990): 35–38.

RANKIN, ELIZABETH D. "Chasing Spotted Horses: The Quest for Human Dignity in Faulkner's Snopes Trilogy." *Faulkner: The Unappeased Imagination. A Collection of Essays.* Ed. Glenn O. Carey. Troy, New York: Whitston, 1980. 139–56.

NOTES

NOTES